Also by I. G. Edmonds

JOEL OF THE HANGING GARDENS

Trickster Tales

Illustrations by Sean Morrison

J. B. LIPPINCOTT COMPANY

Philadelphia   New York

TRICKSTER
TALES

I. G. Edmonds

For Annette
Who Tried to Help

Contents

Trickster Tales

The Tricksters

Do you remember that Saturday morning so long ago when Tom Sawyer had to whitewash the board fence?

Now this was a terrible thing on a spring day when Tom wanted to play instead of work.

The way Mark Twain told it, Tom was unhappily swinging the paint brush when his friend, Ben Rogers, came by. He stopped to tease Tom about having to work on Saturday.

"What do you call work?" Tom said, swinging away with the long-handled brush.

"Why, ain't *that* work?" Ben asked.

"Well, maybe it is, and maybe it ain't. All I know is, it suits Tom Sawyer."

"Oh come, now. You don't mean to let on that you *like* it?"

"Like it? Well, I don't see why I oughtn't to like it. Does a boy get a chance to whitewash a fence every day?"

Ben thought this over and became interested. He begged to be permitted to paint a little. Tom refused, but after Ben offered to give him an apple, he gave in.

Other boys came by, and Tom just as slyly convinced them that painting a fence was much more fun than rafting on the Mississippi River. Of course, each had to pay for the privilege of doing Tom's work for him.

Mark Twain tells us that by the time Tom ran out of whitewash he had gained an apple, a kite, a dead rat and a string to swing it with, a tin soldier, six fire crackers, a dog-collar, and so many more treasures.

And so Tom Sawyer got his work done and was richly paid in the bargain.

Tom Sawyer was a trickster. You will find the trickster in the stories of all countries and all ages. He is the one storybook character who never grows old.

The children of old Egypt at least four thousand years ago laughed at trickster tales. Likewise, when the United States was young, children laughed at the way Benjamin Franklin told how a trickster tricked him into turning a grindstone.

Another famous American trickster was Brer Rabbit.

You remember how he tricked his enemy into throwing him in the briar patch which was just where the wiley rabbit wanted to go. We know this as the famous story of *Brer Rabbit and the Tar Baby* by Joel Chandler Harris, but it really came from Africa where the rabbit was named Wakaima.

As we move around the world, we find trickster tales everywhere. In France the favorite trickster is Reynard-the-Fox. In Mexico children laugh at the tricks played by Don Coyote. Little Turkish boys and girls love the tales of the Hodja, an old teacher who was both silly and very wise at the same time.

In Iran the trickster is Abu Nawas who really lived in the days of the Arabian Nights. From Japan comes tales of Ooka, surely the strangest judge in the world, and Ikkyu, a wise old priest who used tricks to teach lessons. Tyl Eulenspiegel is the German trickster. The jackal is a favorite with children of India.

And so it goes. There are so many it would take weeks to tell them all.

Although their names are different, these famous tricksters were very much alike. In fact, sometimes they tell the same stories about them. Each behaved like a clown, but generally they were very wise men. Their tricks were done mostly to help someone, to teach a lesson, or to make the world a little better place to live in.

But the lessons they teach are not what interest us

here. The lessons are there and that is good, but the important thing is that the world is a gayer, happier place to live because someone—back in the days when storytelling was born—was smart enough to invent the trickster to make us smile forever after.

Here are some of these world-famous trickster tales. They are very old stories and are those actually told in the countries. Wherever I have gone—Thailand, India, Japan, England, France, and other wonderful places—I have always asked people I met to tell me of their local tricksters.

These Trickster Tales are some they have told me . . .

Sissa and the
Troublesome Trifles

Now it happened in the old days that King Balahait was ruler of a province in India. One day he called for his adviser, Sissa.

"Sissa," the king shouted angrily, "it is not possible for a king to do everything himself. He must have advisers to do his work."

"That is true, O Greatest of Kings," Sissa said mildly.

"My other advisers take care of important problems for me," the king went on, his temper growing hotter. "Why don't you do the same?"

"O King, live a thousand years," Sissa said. "I work hard."

"O King, live *two* thousand years," spoke up Rhadama, another of the king's advisers and a man most jealous of Sissa. "Surely Sissa works *hard*, but he never does anything when he works!"

"O King, live *three* thousand years," said Devatta, still another adviser. "Yesterday I inspected the army for you. Rhadama counted your treasure. Indra collected your taxes. But when Sissa was supposed to repair your garden, he wasted his time listening to the complaint of an old begger woman!"

"O King, live *four* thousand years!" spoke up Indra "The day before yesterday, Sissa wasted time looking for a lost child!"

"O King, live *five* thousand years!" Rhadama said, "Sissa is forever wasting time with trifles such as this when he should be worrying about the king's problems."

The king looked at Sissa. "What should I do with you?" he asked, his voice heavy with rage.

"O King, live *six* thousand years," Sissa said. "I do not know what you should do with me."

"What should I do with him?" the king asked the others.

They hesitated. Although they hated Sissa themselves, they knew that the king loved the old man for all his faults. They were afraid to seem too harsh.

"O King, live *seven* thousand years," Indra began slyly. "Why not give Sissa another chance? Then if he fails this last chance, he must be banished."

"That is good advice," the king said. "Rhadama, give Sissa a task to do for me. Let it be something of importance."

"O King, live *eight* thousand years!" the evil adviser said, smothering his glee. "Now it is known that our great king is a lover of peace, but other kings are always fighting him. Let Sissa find a way for all men to live and fight the wars which they must fight without killing anyone!"

"Is that possible?" the king asked. "Oh, I wish it were. I am tired of killings."

"Oh, it must be possible!" the three enemies of Sissa cried together. "We are sure Sissa can do it."

"Fine," the king said. "Sissa, this is your last chance to serve me. Solve this problem and you shall be my Grand Vizier. Fail and I must banish you forever. Since I cannot permit one to leave who knows the palace secrets, I will have no choice but to chop off your head."

The three evil men smiled for they thought Sissa would not be able to solve the problem. "O King, live *forever!*" they cried.

"O King, live forever and a day," Sissa said. "I will go to the mountains and return in a month with the solution."

(7)

"O King, live forever and *two* days—" Indra said. "I——"

"Oh, be quiet!" the king snapped. "I am sick of this live so long business. Rest assured I will live as long as I can. And I don't think your silly wishes will help me at all. Go, Sissa. I expect you back in one month."

Now within a week the evil men reported to the king that their spies claimed that Sissa was not working on the problem at all. Instead the old man was sitting in the shade of a tree, carving little men and animals from ivory while he listened to trifling complaints brought to him by the villagers.

This saddened the king for he really loved his old adviser. However, he had given a king's word that Sissa would be killed if he failed. This could not be changed although the king regretted now that in his anger he had made the promise.

Finally, it was the end of the month. Sissa came back to court. He brought with him the toys he had carved during his stay in the mountains. Gravely he set a checkered board in front of the ruler. Then he placed the little figures upon it. There were tiny castles, war elephants, grand viziers, soldiers, and two kings and two queens. All together they made two armies. One was white ivory. The other was ivory stained black.

"Lord of all the lands!" Sissa said. "Live as long as you wish. On this board which I have named the Royal Game of Chess, men can make war against each other

(8)

without killing. The rules of chess are the same as the rules of war. A leader must play it the same as he would plan his strategy on the battlefield."

"O King!" cried Rhadama. "No game can take the place of real fighting. Sissa is trying to trick us. He has not solved the problem at all. He must be banished. The king has given his royal word."

"I suppose you are right," the king said thoughtfully, looking at the chessboard with interest. "But I would like to try the game myself."

"O King," Sissa said. "I do hear tell that the King of the South is talking of war against our kingdom. Why not try the game with him?"

The king agreed, and sent a challenge to the rival king to meet him on the battlefield of chess.

And it was arranged. The two kings fought across the checkered board for days. They plotted like generals leading armies. They attacked with their foot soldiers. They smashed lines with their elephants. They made sly thrusts with their viziers. And sent their knights charging against the enemy.

But neither could win. Their great battle was a draw. When the rival king saw how closely each was matched with the other in his knowledge of the arts of war, he decided that it would not be wise to attack King Balahait with a real army. The war was called off.

The king was both amazed and overjoyed. He called

his advisers and told them how Sissa's game had indeed permitted them to fight without killing anyone.

Sissa's enemies glowered with rage as the king asked the old man to name his reward.

"Just some rice, O King," Sissa said. "And let it be measured by the chessboard which I have invented. Place one grain of rice on the first of the sixty-four squares of the board. Then place two grains on the second square. Four on the third, doubling each amount until the sixty-four squares are covered."

"Sissa!" the king cried. "How can any man be so wise as to invent chess and so stupid as to ask for such a trifle reward. You have been this way all your life. It was the same when you wasted time from my big problems to listen to the villagers' small ones."

"O King, this is the reward I ask," Sissa said stubbornly.

"Then let it be so," the king said. "I thought you had learned to be wise. I see I was wrong."

Sissa only smiled as the rice was brought. One grain was placed on the first square and swept into a bag for Sissa. Two grains were placed on the second, four on the third, and eight on the fourth. By the time they came to the tenth square it was necessary to measure out 512 grains. This was doubled to make 1024 for the eleventh square. By the time they got to the twentieth square, the amount was over a half million grains.

The king looked uneasy and looked searchingly at Sissa who only smiled.

Soon rice filled all the sacks, covered the floor and ran out the windows.

"How much rice is it going to take to double the amount for sixty-four times?" the alarmed king asked.

"I cannot speak so great a figure," Sissa said, "but I will write it down."

And on the marble wall he wrote: "18,466,744,073,-709,551,615."

The king gasped. "There isn't that much rice in the world! How can such a little thing add up to so much?"

"It is the same with small troubles, O King," Sissa said gently. "All together they are very large even though each may be small in itself. Then they are so great that they can crush a kingdom."

"I see," the king said slowly "I also see now why you spent so much time listening to the small troubles of my people. You have proven to me that I was wrong."

"The king is very wise," Sissa said.

"Now you may ask for another reward for teaching me the value of small things," the king said, "but please, Sissa! Make it a *big* one for rich as I am, I cannot afford another of your *small* rewards!"

"For my other reward I ask only that this rice be given to the poor of the country," the old man said.

"So let it be," the king said. "And as an additional reward, I appoint you my Grand Vizier to see after all

the little problems of the people of my kingdom. You are to see that they do not add up like your doubled grains of rice until they become so big they crush our kingdom."

And it is written that Sissa took the job and did very wisely at it.

[JAPAN]

Ikkyu and the Merchant's Moneybags

Let me tell you of Ikkyu-Osho, the kindly old priest, and the time he carried the greedy merchant's money-bags. The merchant, whose name was Chobei, thought he was tricking Ikkyu, but it seems that this time the trickster got tricked!

Now Ikkyu and Chobei had played together as children in Kyoto, Japan. Even then each tried to get the best of the other. This struggle went on all their lives with each trying to make the other lose "face."

Now it happened on the eve of New Year's Day that

Chobei was out collecting debts owed to him. Just at twilight he saw Ikkyu crossing Kamogawa Bridge.

It had rained that morning and the river was dark with rushing water. Chobei looked at the cold water and smiled slyly as he thought of a plan to embarrass the old priest.

"Ikkyu! My old boyhood friend!" Chobei cried, running up to the old priest. "How lucky that I should meet you here. You see, old friend, I badly need your help."

Ikkyu looked at Chobei and scratched his shaven head as he tried to puzzle out this sudden change in his enemy.

"I am always ready to help the needy," Ikkyu said. "But you are rich."

"Now that is where you are wrong," Chobei said. "A merchant, even when he is doing well, has little money. His wealth is tied up in stock for his store and in debts his customers owe him."

"That sounds reasonable," the old priest said.

"Well, as you know, it is the custom that all Japanese pay their debts by New Year's Day or be disgraced. So I am out collecting from customers who owe me so I can pay the wholesalers from whom I bought my merchandise."

"So?" Ikkyu said. He knew that Chobei was up to some trick, but was not sure what it was. He suspected the river had something to do with it for the merchant looked slyly at the dark water flowing coldly down the stream.

"Well, I have collected some of my money," Chobei said, holding up a well-filled moneybag. "I am now on my way to collect from an old grandmother. I am sure she has no money to pay so I must take her little house and throw her out in the street."

"Oh, and *will* you now?" Ikkyu said softly.

"Oh, yes," Chobei said, not noticing the angry frown on the old priest's face. "Now it will be dark when I return. I am afraid robbers will steal my moneybag. I want you to take it on home for me while I go and dispossess this old woman who cannot pay me."

"Well——" Ikkyu said, and thoughtfully scratched his bald pate.

"It would be an act of charity to an old friend," Chobei said. "Don't you think so, gentlemen?"

This last was said to the crowd who stopped to watch the two old men. They knew how Ikkyu and Chobei were all the time trying to get the better of each other. They wondered which of them would win this time.

"Oh, yes!" they said quickly. "It would be very charitable."

"I don't know——" Ikkyu began doubtfully.

"You are always telling us how we should help others," Chobei said angrily. "Can't you practice what you preach?"

Ikkyu looked unhappy. Then he slowly nodded his

head. "Very well," he said. "I'll carry your money to your home."

"Then you will swear on your honor as a priest that you will carry it home just as I direct?"

"Oh, yes," Ikkyu said carelessly. "I swear."

Chobei laughed gleefully. "Ho! I have the best of you this time, Ikkyu," he cried. "You swore to carry the money to my home as I directed. Then here are my directions: You are not to cross the bridge!"

"But you live on the other side," Ikkyu said. "If I can't cross the bridge, how will I get there?"

"You can wade through the water!" Chobei said. "Or maybe you can think of some other way, being as you are so clever!"

Ikkyu looked at the cold, deep water and shivered. Chobei chuckled. He knew that Ikkyu as a priest could not break his vow. He felt happy at the way he had tricked his old enemy into getting wet this cold evening.

"Very well," Ikkyu said sadly. "I promised to take the money to your house as you directed. So I will not cross the bridge. Give me the moneybag."

"Surely, Chobei," one of the bystanders said, "you are not going to make the old priest wade through the icy water? It is enough that you tricked him. Release him from his promise and we will all admit that you won the battle today."

"Never!" Chobei cried. "Did he feel sorry for me the day he——"

"Please!" Ikkyu said. "Let us not argue. I promised to carry the moneybag as you directed. So be it. Come, give it to me."

Then when Chobei handed it to him, Ikkyu added, "Well, good-by, old childhood friend. I'll see you in six months."

"Six—*what?*" Chobei cried.

"Months," Ikkyu said.

"What do you mean, six months!"

"That is how long it will take me to walk up the river bank to the headwaters and back down the other side."

"But you can't walk around the river!" Chobei cried. "That is six hundred miles!"

"As it happens my old mother lives in the mountains near where the river rises. I have been waiting to visit her anyway."

"Give me my money back! I'm not going to wait six months!"

"Oh, no!" Ikkyu cried. "I made a vow. I *must* carry the money for you."

"I release you from your promise!"

"No! I must carry the money. Who would respect a priest who did not do what he vowed?"

"Then *please* cross the bridge!"

"I cannot!" Ikkyu said. "And I do not intend to get wet this cold day by going through the water."

"Please, Ikkyu! Old friend! If I have to wait six months for my money, I'll be ruined."

"Well," Ikkyu said. "I do not wish to cause you ruin. I think it will keep the terms of our bargain if you carry me through the water on your shoulders."

"But then *I'd* get wet!" Chobei cried. "I'd lose face. Everyone would laugh at *me!*"

"Well," said Ikkyu, "I'll see you in six months."

Tearfully Chobei agreed to carry the old priest through the water. When they got on the other side everyone laughed so hard at Chobei that he grabbed the moneybag and ran home.

So it was that he did not try to collect the debt of the old grandmother. Under the law he could not try to collect again until next New Year's. By that time she had saved enough to pay it.

Everyone praised Ikkyu and laughed at Chobei, the trickster who got tricked!

[ESKIMO]

Agayk and the Strangest Spear

One terrible day when the earth was frozen the ground shook. The ice pack cracked on the sea. The floes piled up, grinding and crushing as the huge slabs of frozen ice heaved up on the shore.

The ice smashed the igloo houses of a little fishing village on the frozen shore. The frightened people fled. In their hurry they forgot Agayk, their medicine man, who was too old to run. That is, all forgot him except the boy, Niklik.

Niklik stayed with the old man. Somehow they

missed death in the crushing ice, but when the earthquake was over, their troubles did not end.

There was nothing to eat. The polar bear, the seal, and even the fish in the sea had run away from the shaking earth even as the people did.

"Make the fish come back," Niklik said to his companion. "I am very hungry."

"That I cannot do," Agayk said sadly.

"But you are a great *shaman*—magician," the boy said. "Don't the people say that a shaman can walk under the water and talk to the fish and whales?"

"The people say that—yes," Agayk replied, his tired old eyes looking sadly at the boy. "But that is a very difficult thing for me to do. I think we must cross the trail over the great ice mountain and fish in the other bay."

"It is so far. Magic is easier."

The magician's dark face, wreathed in the wolverine fur of his parka, looked sad.

"Yes," he said. "Once I was a great medicine man. I was a friend of Raven who flew to the sun and brought back the spark that made the first fire on earth. And I helped the great black bird with his medicine the day a great wave was going to sweep over the land and he turned this wave into *Denali*, the Great One."

He turned and pointed south where the frozen spire of the great mountain the gold seekers would one day call Mount McKinley stuck up high above the land.

"The great bird taught me much magic and medicine, but now I am old and weak. Only the young and strong can make great medicine. This is the way of the world. Raven grew old and left us. The same thing is happening to me."

"Then we will starve," the boy said sadly.

"No, there is fish across the mountains. It is a long way, but we can get there before we starve. Then we have but to cut a hole in the ice and drop in our ivory hooks."

"But the people of the bay are our great enemies," Niklik protested. "They will kill us if we try to fish in their water!"

"Not if we fight them with magic," Agayk replied.

"But you said you were too old to make medicine!"

"I am, but you are young," Agayk said. "You must make the magic."

"I don't know how," Niklik protested.

"I hope I have enough strength left to teach you. Are you willing to learn?"

"Oh, yes!" Niklik said. "Will I be able to walk under the sea and talk to fishes?"

"Well—no," Agayk said. "I am not strong enough to teach you that trick."

"Then maybe you can teach me how to make a fog roll in from the Smokey Sea and hide us. Or will I be able to turn into Nanook the bear and frighten our enemies away?"

"I think the best I can do today is teach you to throw a magic spear."

"Oh, that will be wonderful!" Niklik cried.

"The spear will be made of words."

"Words?" Niklik said uneasily. "That is the strangest spear I ever heard of. Will it work?"

"Because things are as they are—yes, I think so," Agayk said. "Often there is more magic in words than in anything in the world. Had I known this when I was a young man, I would have been an even greater magician than I was."

And so the two climbed the icy trail over the mountain range. It took them five days without food and they were very weak from hunger when they came to the other bay.

There were no fishermen on the ice when they arrived, Niklik chopped a hole in the frozen sea, and dropped an ivory hook into the dark water.

It was night for this was winter and the sun would not shine here above the Arctic Circle for two more months. But the stars were bright and the Northern Lights wove great curtains of soft green, pink, and blue colors through the sky.

This made it as bright as twilight on the ice pack. So it was that they were seen from the shore. All the hunters grabbed their spears and ran to hitch their dogteams. Two got their dogs in the harness first. They

rushed across the ice as if in a mad race to see which could reach the two fishermen first.

"Aiee!" the old medicine man said. "That must be Agarook and Attu. They are the mightiest killers of this village. I have heard it said that they are very jealous of each other. Everytime one does a mighty deed, the other will not sleep until he matches it. They are running a race now to see which will have the honor of killing us."

"Maybe *you* had better use the magic spear," Niklik said uneasily. "They look like very fierce men."

"They are," Agayk admitted. "But the spear would not be powerful enough in my old hands. These men know me. They know I am old and my power gone. Only you can save us now, Niklik-my-son."

"Then give me the spear quickly!" the boy cried.

"They are in these words. When the killers come speak as I tell you."

And the old medicine man then told Niklik what to say. The boy listened, first in surprise and then in alarm.

"We are as good as dead," he said, almost weeping.

"Oh, no," Agayk insisted. "This is good medicine and good magic. Speak as I tell you."

The hunters were almost upon them. Niklik could hear the squeak of the ivory runners as the yelping huskies pulled the racing sleds across the ice pack.

As they came up Agayk pushed back the fur-trimmed

hood of his parka so the two hunters could see his face.

"You are the old shaman from across the icy mountains," Agarook cried. "Why do you steal our fish?"

"Our fish ran when the earth shook," Agayk said.

"I will kill you for stealing our fish," Agarook said.

"No *I* will kill them," Attu said jealously.

"Neither of you will kill us," Agayk said firmly. "We are protected by magic."

"You are old. Your magic is weak," Agarook said.

"That is true," Agayk agreed. "But the boy is young. He will save us with his magic."

The two jealous hunters looked at him in amazement. "The *boy?* Who ever heard of a *boy* medicine man!"

"You have heard of one for I have just told you," Agayk said firmly. "Why the boy is such a great shaman he has secret medicine which will bring the seal from the sea and the bear in from the floes so they can be easily killed."

"Tell me this secret or I will kill you!" Attu cried, pointing the ivory tip of his spear at Niklik's heart.

The boy trembled. His throat was so dry with fear that he had trouble speaking the words which Agayk has assured him had magic hidden in them.

Finally he managed to say: "I can give the secret to only one of you. The secret can only be given to the mightiest hunter."

"I am the mightiest!" Attu cried.

(*27*)

"No!" Agarook shouted. "I am greatest of all!"

"I'll show you who is the mightiest!" Attu cried, raising his spear so it pointed at his enemy instead of the boy Niklik. "Too long you have insulted me with your wild bragging!"

"You are the braggart!" his jealous rival cried, raising his own spear.

All the hatred and jealousy of their years of rivalry boiled over. They started to fight, lunging at each other with their spears.

"Who will win?" Niklik asked Agayk.

"Neither," the old medicine man said. "Each is just as strong as the other. So both must win and both must lose."

"That can't be," Niklik said.

"We'll see," the old shaman said.

As he spoke, each man drove his spear into the other. Both men fell into the fish hole and disappeared under the sea.

Soon the rest of the hunters came up. Surprised at finding the two great hunters gone, they asked where the two were. Agayk told them Niklik had killed them with his magic.

"If a boy can kill such mighty men that even we grown men fear to fight, it must be great magic indeed," their leader said.

"That is right," Agayk said. "He has a magic spear of words. He spoke them and they entered Agarook and

(28)

Attu and in minutes both men were dead. Would you like him to speak the words to you?"

"Oh, no!" the others said.

"Then let us fish in your waters until the fish return to our own bay and I will beg the boy to spare you."

The fearful villagers agreed.

That is how Niklik learned that there is magic in words. With Agayk as his teacher, he grew even wiser in the use of magic talk. So it was that he became a great and famous man among his people, the Eskimo.

Geordie and Ten-Shilling Jock

Aye, laddies, and it were the custom in the old days for a judge to ride out from Glasgow-town to hold court in the villages.

Now the Lords of the Courts were canny men and so they paid the traveling judges no salary. Instead the judges were permitted to keep half of the fines they put upon the people tried in their courts.

You can imagine what happened when a greedy man was made judge. Such a man cared little for justice, but cared a lot for making the fines as large as he could.

Such a rascal was Judge Jock MacKay. No matter how wee the offense, Judge Jock made the fine as large as he could—which as it happened was usually ten shillings. So in time he became known as "Ten-Shilling" Jock and the villagers groaned when he made his round of village courts.

Now it happened one night that Geordie, who had a farm near the Kirk, forgot to fasten his fence. The cow wandered off and when the good people went to the Kirk the next morning, they found Geordie's cow blocking the door so they could not get in to hear the preacher's sermon.

For this Geordie was hailed into Jock's court and fined ten shillings for something which a fairer-minded judge would have only set one shilling.

Now the Englishman likes to say that the Scotsman is a miser. This is not true, although I will admit that our people are a wee bit thrifty. However, to be honest and fair, I must also admit that once in a thousand men there is a Scotsman who is as stingy as the jokers claim.

Geordie was such a man. The loss of a farthing was the loss of a drop of his heart's blood. So it was that the ten-shilling fine made him weep and groan as he swore to get his money back from Ten-Shilling Jock.

Now Jock's next court was to be held on the eighteenth day of the September month, but as the market fair was being held in Glasgow on that day, the court was held one day early.

Now several men were to be tried for small things. Geordie went to see each one. He said that he would like to be their lawyer and would charge them no fee for his service.

Each agreed to let Geordie plead his case. Anyway, a man was always guilty in Ten-Shilling Jock's court.

Geordie insisted only that if he were able to save each man money, he would be given half of what he saved. This was agreed.

So Geordie worked hard in court to prove the accused men innocent. Jock listened with interest, nodded wisely, and then said,

"But a' this is of no matter, laddie. I fine each mon ten shillings."

"Aye and the law says that if a man does not pay his fine he goes to jail." Geordie said quickly. "Aye, then, these men will not pay. Take them to jail."

"Ah!" the judge said, glaring at Geordie. "I see it all now! You are trying to rob me of my fee. You know that there is no jail in this village. The men will have to be taken to Glasgow. You think I do not have time to do this and will let them go free. But no! If I do that every rascal will try the same trick and I'll get no fees. I'll starve. So I will drive them to jail myself in my carriage!"

It was then near sundown and Geordie hastily re-

minded the judge that there were many robbers on the road at night. Jock then decided to wait until morning.

Now the men were very angry at Geordie for having them sent to jail. It was true that this would save them the ten-shillings fine, but the morrow was fair day in Glasgow and each had stuff to sell in the market. They would lose a lot if it could not be sold.

But Geordie only chuckled, "When the sun is high over Glasgow-town, I shall have my ten shillings back!"

So at dawning time Judge Jock loaded the five men in the carriage with him. There was no room for Geordie inside, so he rode on top with the baggage. There was a great deal of this baggage, but Jock was too angry to notice it.

When they reached the jail, Geordie jumped down and cried, "As the lawyer for these men, I have changed their minds. They will pay the ten-shillings fine after all."

"What?" cried the men together. "This man is crazy. First he says this and then he says that! He is not our lawyer anymore."

"When you agreed for him to be your lawyer, you gave him the right to speak for you," the delighted judge said. "Pay the ten shillings!"

The men groaned and cried that they would go to jail first. But they changed their minds when Geordie said slyly, "Pay the fine! And then pay me each of you two

(34)

shillings besides for you promised to pay me half what
I saved for you."

"Aye and you are crazy!" the villagers cried together.
"What have ye saved us, mon?"

"Four shillings!" Geordie cried. "And this is the way I
did it. Now all of you were coming to Glasgow-town to
sell your stuffs at the fair. By the way, your stuffs are in
the bags on top of the coach for I had your wives pack
them for you and I put them aboard.

"Now it so happens that the round-trip fare to Glasgow from our village is fourteen shillings. You get the
round trip for ten for the law says that when a prisoner
is brought to the city for trial the law must also take
him back home if there is no trial. There was none for
you paid your ten-shillings fine.

"Now Jock canno' take you back at once for his
horses are tired and must be rested. That gives you just
time to rush to the fair and make your sales. So you get
a fourteen-shilling trip to the fair for just ten shillings!"

Geordie smiled as the men shouted at Jock's rage.

"Now when each of you pay me two shilling I will
have back the ten Jock took from me," Geordie said.
"At the same time each of you will be two shillings the
better yourself. So everyone gets something except
Jock. Now that is very sad, but *everybody* canno' win,
laddies!"

Hodja and the Jumbled Jobs

Once the great caliph's guards went to the mosque and dragged the hodja before the ruler of Turkey.

"Nasr-ed-Din Hodja!" the caliph cried. "Twice I sent for you. The first time you told my guards you were too stupid to come. The second time you told them you were too wise. And then you turned over and went back to sleep. What do you mean by that?"

"It means that I was sleepy," the hodja said. "Why else would one sleep?"

"Well, you can sleep much better without your

head!" the ruler said pointedly. "For that is what is going to happen to you if you do not do exactly as I tell."

"O Commander of the Faithful, I know I have a very poor head for as many men have told me it is empty as have told me it is full of wisdom," the hodja said, "but it is the only one I have. So I will do exactly as you say."

"Well, I have a great problem. I called in twelve of my wisest advisers. They could not give me an answer. Then I called in twelve of my most foolish advisers. They too failed. So I decided to ask an answer from one who is both wise and foolish. That is you. Give me the answer."

"May Allah prolong the king's life," the hodja said. "I will speak to the twenty-four men who failed and get from them——"

"Very well, if you want to climb down a half mile of steps," the caliph said pleasantly. "I had them put in the deepest dungeon in the palace. I don't like people who fail me."

"Oh," said the hodja. "*Oh!*"

He pushed back his turban and scratched his head. Then he said, "I just happened to remember. This is my foolish day. Perhaps my master—may Allah bring him peace!—should find someone else to advise him on this great problem."

"It is my policy, hodja, that no man be forced to advise me," the caliph said.

(37)

"How very wise," the hodja said, starting to leave. "Every word you speak, O Great Caliph, is a pearl of wisdom."

"So," the caliph went on, "if you do not wish to serve me, you do not have do to so. We will get on with your trial!"

"My—trial?" the hodja said.

"Your trial," the caliph replied. "Did you or did you not pass a house yesterday which had been robbed by a thief?"

"Well—yes," the hodja replied.

"Was or was not the royal executioner about to hang the thief from the doorsill of the house he robbed? Such is our custom."

"It is possible," the hodja said with a sigh.

"And did or did you not stop and say, 'Since this man is too tall to hang from the doorsill, why not pick a short man from the crowd and hang him instead of the tall one!' "

"I—uh—might have," the hodja said. "I was only trying to be helpful. Unfortunately, it happened to be my foolish rather than my wise day."

"So it would seem," said the angry caliph, "for did not everyone laugh so hard at this silly remark that the thief managed to escape?"

"I fear he did," the hodja said sadly.

"And is or is not the law of the land that one who

permits a thief to escape must suffer the missing man's punishment?"

"That is the law," the hodja admitted.

"And are you or are you not short enough to be hanged from this doorway?"

The hodja shivered. "O Great Caliph, may Allah bless your wisdom, what is the task I so foolishly refused to do for you?"

"That is better," the caliph said. "It is a difficult one, but if you can solve it, I might not hold your trial after all."

"Lord, may you live ten thousand years and may I live just as long so I may serve you!"

"Here is the problem," the caliph said. "Many wicked men wish to steal my throne. I hold them off because I have two great chiefs with many warriors who can come to my aid."

"Friendship is the gift of Allah," the hodja said.

"I am not so sure," the caliph replied. "This friendship is the cause of my trouble. Recently my Grand Vizier died. Now each of my friends wishes me to appoint his son to this post. I cannot choose one without offending the other. What shall I do?"

"Give each man a test, and make the one who best performs it your Grand Vizier," the hodja said.

"What kind of a test?" the caliph asked.

"A hodja test," said the hodja.

"Which means," the caliph said grumpily, "that it is

(39)

either a very wise test or a very foolish one. Now remember, these men and their fathers are very jealous. I must do nothing to make them turn against me.

"So be sure your test does not give one an unfair advantage over the other. One of these lads is a fine scholar, but is no warrior. The other is an excellent soldier, but no scholar."

The hodja promised to be careful. He prepared two packages and called the young men to him. "There is a very difficult path up Mount Ararat where Noah landed his Ark so many years ago. The path is hard and takes great strength. It is also difficult to follow and this requires great intelligence. So I have recommended to the Great Caliph that the job of Grand Vizier be given to the one who best shows his strength and intelligence in this climb.

"Now you are to carry nothing with you. Everything you need in the climb is in these two packages. Each of you take one and may Allah go with you. You can go together or you can go separately."

When they had gone, the hodja grinned slyly at the caliph.

"I tricked them," he said. "I made the packages so they will be forced to work together. I put the food in one package and the salt for it in another. And all the rest of the things they need are split the same way. They must share and work together or starve!"

"And what good does this do?" the caliph asked.

"Since one is a scholar and the other is a good soldier, it would be well if they could share the job of Grand Vizier. The scholar could handle the laws for you and the soldier could direct your army."

"Hodja!" the caliph cried. "This must be one of your foolish days. I'll admit that your trick will force the two men to work together on the mountain climb for it is all rock after they pass the timberline. But when they come back here there will be nothing to force them to get along. Then they will be at each other's throats with knives if I try to make them work together."

"Well, maybe they will come back on one of my wise days and I'll think of something."

"I hope so for your sake, hodja," the caliph said. "While it will grieve me to have your head chopped off, still I have no choice. It is the custom for caliphs to treat their advisers this way when they fail a job. And you certainly wouldn't want me to break a custom would you?"

"Oh, I wouldn't mind at all!" the hodja said quickly.

"Well, I would!" the caliph snapped.

"Then I will pray to Allah to give me wisdom," the little hodja said.

And in a few days the two men returned from the difficult climb up the rocky cliffs of Mount Ararat. They came to the palace with their fierce old fathers.

"Well, hodja?" the caliph said angrily. "What are you going to do? You promised to choose one of the young

men and do it in such a manner that their fathers will not get angry."

"What am I going to do?" the hodja repeated.

"That is what *I* am asking *you!*" the caliph said with an angry glare at the little teacher—for that is what the word hodja means.

The hodja thoughtfully pushed back his turban so he could scratch his head. He sighed and said, "As fathers you would feel very bad if your sons failed to do a good job."

Each angrily claimed that his son would make a splendid Grand Vizier.

"And will you agree that the caliph should put them to death if they fail to do a good job?" the hodja asked slyly.

When the men agreed that this was just, the hodja said to the soldierly young man, "In the name of the caliph I appoint you Grand Vizier to make the laws, keep the records, and check on clerks."

"But I know nothing of such work," the young man protested. "I am a soldier. I should——"

"This young man understands such things," the hodja said. "He can help you as he helped you on the mountain climb."

"Never," the outraged scholar cried. "On the mountain we worked together to save our lives. It is not so now. Why should I help him?"

The hodja thoughtfully scratched his head again.

"Well, now that you ask me," he said, "I can think of only one reason. That is, because you will need his advice to help you run the army and protect the kingdom for I am appointing you Grand Vizier in that position."

"But——!" both young men and their fathers cried.

"You have these jobs in the caliph's name and your fathers have sworn on the Holy Koran that you may be put to death if you don't do the job well.

"You worked together on the mountain because you had to do so. That is why I sent you there. To prove to you that you could get along when you have to. Now you have to do so again."

And so since they had to, they had to help each other. In time they became friends and made the caliph good and true servants.

And all through the jewel city men said the hodja was the wisest foolish man in the kingdom.

[GERMANY]

Tyl's Task

His Honor, the *burgomeister* of a town near Bremen, was sitting before his fireplace. His feet were stretched out comfortably on a huge bear rug, and he was gnawing on a chicken leg.

The servant girl came to the door to tell him that Tyl Eulenspiegel was outside.

"That rascal!" His Honor cried, almost choking on the chicken leg. "He is out to trick me again. What did the scoundrel say he wanted?"

"The house of a poor man burned last night," she said. "Tyl is collecting money to help rebuild it."

"And he expects to get it from *me?*" His Honor cried.

(45)

"I did not get rich by throwing money away. Not one *mark* will this rascal get from me!"

"But, master, it will look bad if everyone gives except the *burgomeister*," she said.

"Ah! I shall give, but it will be Tyl Eulenspiegel's money I give! At last I see a way to repay that rascal for the tricks he has played on me. People will not think him so sly when I am finished with him. They will think that *I* am the smart one. Show him in. I am ready for Tyl Eulenspiegel this time!"

When Tyl came into the room he was surprised at the jovial way his enemy greeted him.

"Ho, Tyl!" cried the burgomeister. "So you want some money?"

"Yes," Tyl said, explaining that the collections would be used to help the unfortunate.

"Well, Tyl, you know that I love a game. So let us make a game of this, eh? I will ask you three questions. If you cannot answer, you pay for me, eh?"

"Well, now——" Tyl began.

"This way the good people can see which of us is smarter, eh?" the burgomeister said.

"I'll do it," Tyl replied without bothering to find out what the questions were. It is very sad to relate, but Tyl had gotten the best of his old enemy so many times that he thought he could not lose.

"Well, now," said the burgomeister, delighted. "Here is the first question: What am I thinking?"

(46)

"That is easy," Tyl said. "You think you will fool me, but you will not."

"Oh?" said the burgomeister. "We will let the two remaining questions decide if you are right or wrong about that. Here is your next question: How many hairs are there on my head!"

"I——" Tyl began and stopped. His neck got a little red and for the first time he started to worry that the burgomeister had at last gotten the better of him. He groaned, thinking how everyone had laughed at the burgomeister the last time Tyl got the best of him. Now Tyl could see everyone laughing at him.

"Well——" he said, deciding to make a guess and hoping his luck would make it right. "About——"

"About, nothing!" the other man snapped. "You must give me the correct number right to the last one."

"The last—one——" Tyl said. Then his face brightened. "One! Ah! That gives me an idea."

He went over and pulled one hair from the head of the surprised burgomeister. "Ouch!" said His Honor.

"Now," Tyl said with a smile. "You wanted to know how many hairs there are in your head. There is exactly one less than there was before! Next question please."

"You—you——!" the outraged official said. "You will not trick me again. "How many stars are there in the sky! You have one minute to answer."

"Well——!" Tyl began and stopped.

"Ha! I have you now," the burgomeister cried. "Pay the money for me—Oops!"

This last he said when in his haste he tripped over the great bearskin rug at his feet. He almost fell.

Tyl laughed and the other man said angrily, "Are you laughing at my misfortune?"

"No," Tyl said. "I am laughing at my stupidity. You see I had forgotten that the number of the stars in the sky is exactly the same as the number of hairs in your bearskin rug."

"You are trying to trick me again!" the burgomeister cried. "They are not the same!"

"But it is so," Tyl insisted. Then his smile faded and he said somewhat shamefacedly, "No, I was wrong."

"Ha! Pay the money for me."

"Not yet," Tyl said. He stooped and pulled one hair from the rug. "I forgot that there was a falling star last night. Now the number is correct. You lose."

"Impossible!" his old enemy cried.

"Then call your servants and have them count the hairs on this bearskin rug and the stars in the sky," Tyl said. "If I am not right I will pay your part of the money to rebuild the old man's house and buy you a new suit of clothes to boot."

"That's a bet!" the delighted official cried.

"And if I am right, you will pay the money and buy me a fine linen suit?"

"Yes, yes! Hans! Gerta! Come quickly and start counting."

"It will, of course, take them about three years," Tyl said with a smile.

"You mean I must lose the work of two servants for three years just to win three *marks* from you?"

"No, *six* years," Tyl said. "They must count the stars after they finish with the rug."

"It is cheaper to pay," the burgomeister said with a groan. "Tyl, you have tricked me again. But you just wait until *next* time!"

[IRAN (Persia)]

The Just Judgment

I

Heroes should win. That is the way things are. But poor Abu-al-Nawas—that great hero of Old Bagdad—lost as often as he won. This may have been because he was right only half the time.

Anyway, it happened in the years when Haroun-al-Raschid—on whom be peace—was caliph of Bagdad that the Commander of the Faithful became very angry at his old friend Abu.

It seems that Haroun set up Abu as a judge over the poor people of Bagdad. This was a great job and a greater honor for the name Haroun-al-Raschid means Aaron the Just and the caliph was as just as his name. He put great store by justice and picked only the men he trusted most as his judges.

(51)

Sad to relate, however, Abu-al-Nawas was a lazy man. Oh, he was generous of heart and a gay fellow, but he did not like to work. Many times this made Haroun very angry, but somehow Abu always managed by his wit to turn the caliph's anger to laughter.

So it was that Abu celebrated his new job by dancing and singing all night. When dawn came, instead of holding court, he crept off to his silken pillows to sleep.

He had no sooner dropped off to sleep than he was awakened by men crying for justice.

"This," said Abu with a groan, "will never do. Do these rascals think I intend to lose sleep over their petty problems? Nay! A sly fellow like me will stop this nonsense at once."

He rolled sleepily from his great pillow bed and pointed to the first man in line. "What is your complaint?" he said. "Speak quickly for the justice of Abu-al-Nawas is like an old woman's tongue. It moves rapidly."

"Lord," said the first man, "this rascal took a sword to kill his sheep. He missed his stroke and cut off the tail of my goat. I asked him to pay for the lost tail. He refused. I want my money."

"Oh?" said Abu with a yawn. "A goat's tail is such a small thing to pay for. So here is my judgment: The man who cut off the tail of your goat must take the goat home with him and keep it until it grows a new tail for you!"

"But—but——!" the outraged man cried. "But goats

can't grow new tails!"

"Tell the goat I said to try," Abu replied. "Next case."

There were none. The others fled from the palace. No one wanted this kind of justice. This pleased Abu who went back to sleep.

II

Now within the hour the tale of this strange justice came to the ear of the great caliph—May he live ten thousand years! Haroun shook with wrath and called for his milk-white horse. He mounted and rode furiously through the streets of the pearl of cities until he came to the palace where Abu-al-Nawas lived as a judge.

He found Abu still asleep. He knew from experience how the sly man could slip out of trouble. So he decided to trap his false judge. So changing his voice, the caliph said, "It is the caliph's orders that all men have justice. Awake and give me a judgment."

Abu groaned and rolled over. The light hurt his eyes and he hid his head under a pillow.

"I thought I taught these rascals not to bother me when I'm sleepy," he muttered.

Haroun's face turned purple with rage, but he only said, "I want justice as the Great Caliph promised."

"Well, what is your problem?" Abu asked, not taking his head from under the pillow.

"I have a servant who has done me wrong," Haroun said, glaring at the body of Abu stretched out on his pillows.

"Then harken to the judgment of Abu-al-Nawas, the world's wisest man," Abu said. "It is natural for servants to do wrong to their masters. Why I often do wrong to my master the Great Caliph. So what is natural cannot be a crime for that is the way things are done. You are at fault for bringing such a small matter to disturb the court. Therefore I sentence you to go home and work hard to make more money so your servant will have more to steal. Now go away and let me sleep."

Haroun-al-Raschid could contain his rage no longer. "Abu!" he shouted. "You ten-thousand-times-condemned rascal! Is this what you call *justice?*"

The startled judge rolled off his pillows and bumped his head on the marble floor to show his respect for the Great Caliph.

"Welcome, O Commander of the Faithful," he cried. "May you live ten thousand years. I see you were taken in by the little joke I devised to make the day more pleasant for my master who *loves* little *jokes!*"

"Abu, I do like jokes, but I do not like the caliph's justice mixed with jokes. This time you have gone too far."

"My Lord," Abu said boldly, "I am only an ignorant slave. You were at fault for making such a one as me into a judge. And I am still the caliph's judge although I think you are going to remove me. So while I am still judge I make my last judgment: I judge you guilty for making me a judge!"

"Abu," Haroun said, "you are right. I was at fault. You did not understand that justice is the greatest gift of God to man. So I forgive you and remove you as a judge."

"Oh, thank you, Great Caliph, may you live ten times ten thousand-thousand years. I will now go back to my sleep."

"Oh, no! I forgave you because you did not understand justice. *Now* you understand it. So I am reappointing you judge. And just so you will not forget what justice means in Bagdad, I shall have the royal swordsman stand right behind you with his scimitar each time you hand down a judgment. You *know* what he will *do* with his sword if *you* don't give a *good* decision!"

III

Now as the street was packed with men seeking justice, Haroun forced Abu to go to the balcony and hold court. Haroun stood on one side of his unhappy judge and the royal swordsman on the other.

"You be sure, Abu, that *everybody* gets what he deserves," Haroun said. "Or—*else!*"

Abu looked at the sharp scimitar in the hands of the swordsman and shivered.

He shivered even more when he heard the first case for it seemed one in which it would be impossible for both sides to get what they deserved.

What happened was that a rich moneylender demanded that an old man, who could not repay a loan, should give up his mud hut and goats in payment.

Now under the law the moneylender deserved his money. But, if the old man gave up his hut and goats, he would starve. He certainly did not deserve that.

Abu gulped. "If I give the moneylender what he deserves, the old man will get what he does not deserve," he said to Haroun-al-Raschid.

"That is right," the still angry caliph said.

"But you said—and every word you utter is a pearl of great price, O Great Master of Bagdad—that each must get what he deserves. That is impossible in this case."

"Abu, do you remember the time my gold bowl vanished when only you and a little mouse were in the room. You denied stealing it and claimed the mouse *ate* it. I said that such a thing was impossible. And you said, 'Nothing is *impossible.*' Do you remember?"

"Well, *maybe,*" Abu said reluctantly.

"Well, now I say 'Nothing is impossible' and I *don't* say maybe. Give each man what he deserves or—so help me—you will get what you have long deserved!"

"Maybe," said Abu to the moneylender, "you could agree to wait a little while for your money."

"He will never have any," the moneylender said. "I want everything he owns. Even that will not pay all my interest."

"*Everything?*" Abu said, looking surprised and then pleased. "You shall have it! That is the judgment of Abu-al-Nawas. Do you accept it?"

"Yes, yes," the greedy moneylender said quickly. "Give me *everything!*"

"Abu!" Haroun said. "This is not a good judgment. I warned you."

"But he deserves *everything*, O Great Caliph. And he shall get it. Take the old man's house. Take the old man's goats. Take the old man's wife——"

"But, great judge," the moneylender protested. "I do not want the wife. She is fat and has the temper of two dragons."

"Nevertheless, you are going to get everything and she is part of that. You can also have his daughter——"

"But, great judge, she has a face like a camel and is even worse tempered than her mother. I could never get her married to anyone. I would have to feed her all her life!"

"When you get everything, you get everything," Abu said stubbornly.

"Also," Abu added, "he has a son as well. The boy is now yours."

"But he is lame and cannot work!"

"Also I notice the old man has rheumatism. You can have that, too."

"But how can I take his sickness?"

"That is your worry," said Abu. "But if the court awards you this, then you must take it for an order is an order."

"Oh, woe is me!" cried the moneylender. "What kind of justice is this?"

"The justice of Abu," the judge replied. "And now we must insure that Hassen the old man gets what he deserves since you have now gotten what you deserve— which is everything. I think Hassen deserves some time to prepare himself to give you his all. Will you permit him some time?"

"How much time?" the frightened moneylender asked.

"As much as you want to give him," Abu said.

"He can wait ten thousand years!"

"No," said Abu with a smile. "That would be too long and it would rob you of the gold which you loaned Hassen. Give him just a few minutes. I think that will be enough for I have noticed that when his judges make a very brilliant decision it is the custom of our

Great Caliph—on whom be peace!—to reward the judge with a little sack of gold.

"Now since I have done very brilliantly here, I am sure he will do the same to me. When he does I will give it to Hassen who will then pay you what he owes."

And that is the way it happened. Everyone got what he deserved and everyone was very happy. Except Abu —that is. Haroun-al-Raschid was so pleased with his decision that he made Abu remain a judge. And just to make sure that the lazy al-Nawas did not spend his time in bed, he left the royal swordsman to keep him company.

And history records that Abu—simply because he had to—was a very wise judge. He wasn't happy, but he made very many other people happy in Bagdad. All of which greatly pleased Haroun-al-Raschid who believed that justice is the greatest of all gifts.

[JAPAN]

Ooka and the Telltale Tale

Now it happened in the old days of Japan that there was a judge named Ooka who was a great trickster. Why, they tell tales of how he brought a tree into court as a witness, accused a stone statue of being a thief, and did any number of strange things.

All these tricks he used to find out the truth and put guilty people in jail. One of his tricky cases was called the Telltale Tale.

It happened when there was a bold robbery of a shop owned by an old man and his wife. They saw the robber run out of the store that night and Ooka thought it would be simple for them to recognize the thief.

Sad to relate, it turned out not to be easy at all. There were two suspects and they looked enough alike to be twins. The old man and his wife could not decide which one it was they saw.

So Ooka put many tricky questions to the two men, hoping the thief would make a mistake. The robber was too smart.

Ooka sighed and his ears got a little red as they always did when he was embarrassed. Sad to relate, he was very proud of the way he could trick the guilty into confessing and it embarrassed him greatly whenever he failed.

He sat for a long time looking at the two men before him. Finally he said, "When I was a child my grandfather told me that if one stirs muddy water it will only get darker, but if one lets it stand still, the mud will settle and the water will become clear.

"So that is what we will do here. We will sit and wait for the muddy water of this case to clear. Then I will easily see the truth."

And so they sat for a long time and everyone in the courtroom got very tired of just sitting. The judge was very strict. He would not let them talk or scarcely move.

Ooka waited slyly until he was sure all were so tired they could scarcely move. Then he said, "I am sorry, but the muddy water is not yet clear. But if it will help lighten the hours while we wait, we will hear some stories."

He pointed his fan at Jiroemon, one of the two accused men.

"You tell us a story first," Ooka said. "Tell us about the cleverest man you ever heard of."

"Yes, honorable honor," Jiroemon said, bowing low as is fitting and proper when speaking to so great a judge.

"I think the cleverest man I ever knew was the farmer Nakamura. This man who lives near me raises rabbits to help feed his family. One night one of his fattest hares disappeared. The next night another and another. He tried all sorts of traps, but could not catch the thief.

"He complained to the police, but they could not find the robber either. Then when another rabbit disappeared, he knew he had to do something himself or he would lose them all to this clever thief."

"So the thief was clever, was he?" Ooka asked, his face, showing great interest in the story.

"Oh, yes, honorable honor," the taleteller said, "but as I will relate, he was not so clever as farmer Nakamura.

"Nakamura-san had a friend who is the village schoolteacher. He went to this teacher and asked if he would have the children, as their lesson for the day, write about what they had to eat that week.

"His friend agreed and when he graded the lesson

papers he found that all the little boys and girls had written about eating rice and vegetables except one child, the son of a lazy man named Zensuke. He told about the rabbit stew he had to eat!

"And so it was that Nakamura-san knew who had stolen his rabbits. He went to the police who brought the thief to jail."

"That is a very good story about a very clever man," Ooka said. "It also is a story that teaches me something."

"And what is that, honorable honor?" Jiroemon asked.

"*That* I will speak of in due time," the judge replied. "Now we must not keep the next storyteller waiting. You there, Uhei, now it is your turn. Tell us of the cleverest man you ever met.

The second accused bowed in a manner fitting and proper to the great judge's rank and said, "O, honorable honor, I think it must have been Gompachi, the famous thief. Once I heard how this sly man got two treasures from only one robbery. Now that is very sly indeed."

"And so it is, indeed, indeed," Ooka said and his usually grave face lighted up in a happy smile. "Tell us more and be quick for this is a tale that interests me greatly."

"Yes, O great judge," Uhei said, pleased that the judge liked his story so well. "It happened thus: Gompachi and another thief named Onoei were arguing over who was the cleverest thief. Gompachi said that he was because he was clever enough to steal the silk sheets off the bed of the Mayor of Meguro while his honor was sleeping on them.

"Now Onoei knew such a thing was impossible. So he offered to bet Gompachi that it could not be done.

" 'I have just robbed a merchant of ten pieces of gold. I will bet all of them that you cannot steal the sheets from under a sleeping man—not a very fat man like the mayor,' Onoei said.

"Gompachi agreed to the bet—and do you know, honorable honor! He *did* it! And this is how this clever man worked. He slipped into the mayor's home that night. He carried a chicken feather which he used to gently tickle the mayor's back. His honor groaned and rolled over sleepily. Gompachi then neatly folded up one side of the sheet so it was next to the mayor's body. Then he slipped around on the other side and tickled the mayor with the chicken feather. His honor groaned sleepily and rolled over so that he lay off the folded sheet. Gompachi then slipped from the house with the silk sheet. He sold it for one piece of silver and got the ten pieces of gold from his bet. So you can see how this clever man was rewarded twice!"

"That," said Ooka, "is a tale of a very clever man indeed—oh, yes indeed, but I do not think either he or farmer Nakamura are so clever as the man I will tell

you all about. This man is the Judge Ooka—a most clever man, if you will pardon my saying so. You see, this judge was once given a case which he could not solve at all. The truth is that the only two possible suspects looked so much alike that the witnesses could not tell which one they saw running from their little store after it was robbed.

"Since he could not discover which was the thief, this judge had to try a little trick. What he did was have each of the two suspects tell a story about the cleverest man he knew. Now he did this because he knew that an honest man would hate a thief, but that a robber would like a thief like himself.

"Now in the two stories he had the two suspects tell, one told about an honest man who tricked a thief. The other told about a thief who used a trick to steal from an honest man. So therefore——"

But before he could finish, Uhei who told the story of the clever thief, jumped up and tried to escape from the courtroom. Ooka's servants ran after him. They caught him in the street and dragged him off to jail.

Inside the great judge smiled at the people in the court.

"It seems," he said, "that the muddy water is now clear. We can all go home and be thankful that justice has won again."

[GREECE]

The Silly Slave

Once in Ephesus in the land of Greek Ionia there was a rich merchant who had a hard time finding a teacher for his children. When he found a man wise enough to teach the morals he wanted his boys to learn, the man was so dull that he put the children to sleep in the classroom.

On the other hand the teachers he found who were lively and told interesting stories were not wise enough to teach the moral lessons this man—Iedmon was his name—insisted on his children learning.

So it was that he went to the great slave market just back of the Temple of Diana of the Ephesians.

"Slavemaster," he said to the man who sold slaves, "I

badly need a wise, but interesting, teacher for my young sons. I will pay many gold pieces for such a man. Also, if he can teach as I want my children taught, I will be so grateful that at the end of one year I will set the slave free."

Now when they heard this, all the slaves wanted very much to be the one chosen by Iedmon. They all started to shout and tell him how very wise they were.

That is, all shouted except one. He was a little man, scarcely larger than a child, but his face was so ugly it was funny. He looked so silly that the others called him the Little Clown Slave.

They were wrong in thinking him foolish. Behind his silly mask of a face he was one of the wisest men who ever lived.

He did not, of course, know how really wise he was, but he knew that he was much smarter than the other slaves in the market. He also knew that his silly face would cause Iedmon to pass him by unless he could do something to convince the rich merchant that he really was a wise teacher.

So while the others shouted to *tell* Iedmon how wise they were, the little slave sat back planning how he could *show* the merchant that he was wiser than they.

"I think," he told himself, "that I had best tell him some of my little stories. Then he can see how I would teach his sons by telling them stories which they could love but which would also teach them a lesson."

Carefully he picked out a few of his stories that had good lessons to teach. The first proved that it is unwise to tell a lie just to be funny.

It was about a boy who loved to play tricks. He was a shepherd lad who tended flocks on the hills above Old Athens. One day he thought it would be a funny trick to frighten the other shepherds. So he ran down the hill shouting:

"Wolf! Wolf! A wolf is eating the sheep!"

The other shepherds came running to kill the wolf and the trickster laughed very hard. He thought this very funny. But the very next day a real wolf attacked the flocks. He ran down the hill shouting:

"Help! Help! Wolf! Wolf! A wolf is eating my sheep!"

This time no one came to help for they thought he was trying to trick them again. He lost all his sheep because he told a lie just to be funny.

The little slave also picked out two other stories to tell as well, which gave lessons in generosity and thrift.

While he was planning these stories, Iedmon was going through the pens, testing the wisdom of different men. Finally he came to the little slave.

"O great master!" the little slave cried. "Let me tell you a wonderful t-t-t-t-t——"

(70)

He was so excited at the thought of earning his freedom that the words stuck in his throat.

He stopped and tried to start again.

"L—l-l-let me t-t-t-t-t——"

He just couldn't stop his stuttering. A tear squeezed out of his eye and plopped off the end of his ridiculous nose. He looked so funny in his misery that the others started to laugh loudly.

The little slave took a deep breath and started again. This time he forced himself to talk slowly. The words came out beautifully and very wise.

But Iedmon passed on. The noise of the laughter was so great that he did not hear a single word of the tale of the boy who cried wolf.

Iedmon did not find the kind of teacher he wanted. So each time that new slaves were brought to Ephesus he came down to search again. The little slave always tried to attract his attention, but Iedmon, remembering the other time, would not listen to him.

Finally it happened one day that Iedmon needed to carry a lot of goods up-country to Sardis, the great city of Croesus, the richest man in the world.

He rented a lot of slaves from the market to carry his bundles. The little slave was one of these.

The merchandise had been piled beside Iedmon's warehouse when the slaves were marched over to get it. The merchant came out to give orders to the slave-master. As the two passed by him, the little slave looked slyly at his companions and then shouted loud enough for Iedmon to hear:

"Quickly!" he cried. "Some of the bundles are small and some are large. The last ones to pick them up will have to carry the big ones! Quickly! Let's get the small ones!"

It was a long way to Sardis and all were eager to get the lighter loads. They all rushed forward. The little slave was the fastest one of them all. He was the first to reach the bundles.

But instead of grabbing the smallest, he chose the largest of them all—a woven reed basket filled with something covered by cloth covers.

"I win! I win!" he cried triumphantly.

The others laughed at his silliness. Iedmon shook his head.

"I am not sure," he said to the slavemaster, "that I want anyone that silly carrying my goods. He might harm them."

"I will watch him very closely, master," said the overseer.

"But I am not silly at all!" the little slave cried. "I was smarter than all the others!"

"Oh?" said Iedmon. "How do you think that? You had your choice of all the bundles, but you passed up the small ones and took instead the biggest of the lot."

(72)

"That was because I am wiser than they," the slave said stubbornly.

Iedmon looked at the slavemaster. "He is crazy."

"Oh, no," the little slave said. "When I saw the bundles were of a different size, I asked myself why it should be so. Then I decided that the packers had made some small because their contents were very heavy—maybe of iron—so that a man could not carry a larger load.

"Then I asked myself why one basket should be so large and I told myself that it was because what was inside was lighter than the smaller bundles.

"Then I saw the breeze gently lift up one corner of the cloth covering the basket and discovered that it had bread inside.

"Now I knew that although some bundles were large and some were small, they were about the same weight for the packers would try to make everyone's load equal.

"But I also knew that we slaves would be fed at noon and that this bread would be our meal. So by taking the largest of them all, I got no larger load than the others, but at noon my load would be all gone and I would have nothing to carry all afternoon! The rest would still have their heavy loads all the way to Ephesus!"

Iedmon smiled. "You are quite a trickster," he said. "Since you will have nothing to carry, I suppose you will help one of your friends."

(74)

"Oh, no," the slave replied. "If I helped one, I would help only one. I shall help them all. You see, O great master, I tell very fine stories. And as I walk along this afternoon, I shall tell them to my companions and it will take their minds off their burdens. That way I will help them all."

"Well!" said Iedmon. "You are wiser than I thought."

"That is true, O great master," the little slave said. "I know that I look like a silly fool, but I am wise and I love to teach my fellow man. Since I do look like a clown, none will listen to me when I say wise things. So I have hidden them in my stories. They think I only speak to amuse them, but my stories teach lessons as well. Would you like to hear one?"

"That I would," Iedmon said thoughtfully, "but there is not time now. We must start for Sardis if we are to deliver King Croesus' goods on time. So I tell you what we will do. I will have another slave hired to carry the bread. You will walk beside me and tell me one of those wise stories of yours."

This the little slave did and Iedmon was so impressed with his wisdom that he bought him from the slave dealer. Unfortunately for Iedmon he never got to use the slave for a teacher of his sons. He bragged about his wisdom to King Croesus and the king insisted on having the wise little slave for his own. Iedmon could not refuse to sell him to the king.

The king was so delighted with the slave's stories that he made him a free man.

This is not all the story for the little trickster's tales still teach us today. He was Aesop who wrote the Fables.

Señor Coyote and the Tricked Trickster

One day long ago in Mexico's land of sand and giant cactus *Señor* Coyote and *Señor* Mouse had a quarrel.

None now alive can remember why, but recalling what spirited *caballeros* these two were, I suspect that it was some small thing that meant little.

Be that as it may, these two took their quarrels seriously and for a long time would not speak to each other.

Then one day Mouse found Señor Coyote caught in a trap. He howled and twisted and fought, but he could not get out. He had just about given up when he saw Señor Mouse grinning at him.

"Mouse! *Mi viejo amigo*—my old friend!" he cried. "Please gnaw this leather strap in two and get me out of this trap."

"But we are no longer friends," Mouse said. "We have quarreled, remember?"

"Nonsense!" Señor Coyote cried. "Why I love you better than I do Rattlesnake, Owl, or anybody in the desert. You must gnaw me loose. And please hurry for if the *peon* catches me I will wind up a fur rug on his wife's kitchen floor."

Mouse remembered how mean Señor Coyote had been to him. He was always playing tricks on Mouse and his friends. They were very funny to Señor Coyote for he was a great trickster, but often they hurt little Mouse.

"I'd like to gnaw you free," he said, "but I am old and my teeth tire easily."

"Really, Señor Mouse, you are ungrateful," said Señor Coyote reproachfully. "Remember all the nice things I have done for you."

"What were they?"

"Why——" Coyote began and stopped. He was unable to think of a single thing. There was good reason for this. He had done nothing for Mouse but trick him.

But Señor Coyote is a sly fellow. He said quickly,

"Oh, why remind you of them. You remember them all."

"I fear my memory of yesterday is too dim," Mouse said, "but I could remember very well what you could do for me tomorrow."

"Tomorrow?" Coyote asked.

"Yes, tomorrow. If I gnaw away the leather rope holding you in the trap, what will you do for me tomorrow, and the day after tomorrow and the day after the day after tomorrow and the day——"

"Stop!" Señor Coyote cried. "How long is this going on?"

"A life is worth a life. If I save your life, you should work for me for a lifetime. That is the only fair thing to do."

"But everyone would laugh at a big, brave, smart fellow like me working as a slave for a mere mouse!" Señor Coyote cried.

"Is that worse than feeling sad for you because your hide is a rug in the peon's kitchen?"

Señor Coyote groaned and cried and argued, but finally agreed when he saw that Mouse would not help him otherwise.

"Very well," he said tearfully, "I agree to work for you until either of us die or until I have a chance to get even by saving your life."

Mouse said with a sly grin, "That is very fine, but I remember what a great trickster you are. So you must

(79)

also promise that as soon as I free you that you will not jump on me, threaten to kill me, and then save my life by letting me go!"

"Why, how can you suggest such a thing!" Coyote cried indignantly. And then to himself he added, "This mouse is getting *too* smart!"

"Very well, promise," Mouse said.

"But I am not made for work," Señor Coyote said tearfully. "I live by being sly."

"Then be sly and get out of the trap yourself," Mouse retorted.

"Very well," Señor Coyote said sadly. "I will work for you until I can pay back the debt of my life."

And so Mouse gnawed the leather strap in two and Coyote was saved. Then for many days thereafter Señor Coyote worked for Mouse. Mouse was very proud to have the famous Señor Coyote for a servant. Señor Coyote was greatly embarrassed since he did not like being a servant and disliked working even more.

There was nothing he could do since he had given his promise. He worked all day and dreamed all night of how he could trick his way out of his troubles. He could think of nothing.

Then one day Baby Mouse came running to him. "My father has been caught by Señor Snake!" he cried. "Please come and save him."

"Hooray!" cried Coyote. "If I save him, I will be released from my promise to work for him."

He went out to the desert rocks and found Señor Rattlesnake with his coils around Señor Mouse.

"Please let him go and I will catch you two more mice," Coyote said.

"My wise old mother used to tell me that a bird in hand is worth two in the bush," Snake replied. "By the same reasoning, one mouse in Snake's stomach is worth two in Coyote's mind."

"Well, I tried, Mouse," Coyote said. "I'm sorry you must be eaten."

"But you must save me, then you will be free from your promise to me," Mouse said.

"If you're eaten, I'll be free anyway," Coyote said.

"Then everyone will say that Coyote was not smart enough to trick Snake," Mouse said quickly. "And I think they will be right. It makes me very sad for I always thought Señor Coyote the greatest trickster in the world."

This made Coyote's face turn red. He was very proud that everyone thought him so clever. Now he just *had* to save Mouse.

So he said to Snake, "How did you catch Mouse anyway?"

"A rock rolled on top of him and he was trapped," Mouse said. "He asked me to help him roll it off. When I did he jumped on me before I could run away."

"That is not true," Snake said. "How could a little mouse have the strength to roll away a big rock. There

is the rock. Now you tell me if you think Mouse could roll it."

It was a very big rock and Coyote admitted that Mouse could not possibly have budged it.

"But it is like the story *Mamacita* tells her children at bedtime," Mouse said quickly. "Once there was a poor burro who had a load of hay just as large as he could carry. His master added just one more straw and the poor burro fell in the dirt. Snake did not have quite enough strength to push the rock off himself. I came along and was like that last straw on the burro's back and together we rolled the rock away."

"Maybe that is true," Snake said, "but by Mouse's own words, he did only a very little of the work. So I owe him only a very little thanks. That is not enough to keep me from eating him."

"Hmmm," said Coyote. "Now you understand, Snake, that I do not care what happens myself. If Mouse is eaten, I will be free of my bargain anyway. I am only thinking of your own welfare, Snake."

"Thank you," said Señor Rattlesnake, "but I do enough thinking about my welfare for both of us. I don't need your thoughts."

"Nevertheless," Coyote insisted, "everyone is going to say that you ate Mouse after he was kind enough to help you."

"I don't care," Snake said. "Nobody says anything good of me anyway."

"Well," said Coyote, "I'll tell you what we should do. We should put everything back as it was. Then I will see for myself if Mouse was as much help as he said he was or as little as you claim. Then I can tell everyone that you were right, Snake."

"Very well," said Señor Snake. "I was lying like this and the rock was on me——"

"Like this?" Coyote said, quickly rolling the rock across Snake's body.

"Ouch!" said Snake. "That is right."

"Can you get out?" Coyote asked.

"No," said Snake.

"Then turn Mouse loose and let him push," said Coyote.

This Snake did, but before Mouse could push, Coyote said, "But on second thought if Mouse pushes, you would then grab him again and we'd be back arguing. Since you are both as you were before the argument started, let us leave it at that and all be friends again!"

Then Coyote turned to Mouse. "So, my friend, I have now saved your life. We are now even and my debt to you is paid."

"But mine is such a *little* life," Mouse protested. "And yours is so much *larger*. I don't think they balance. You should still pay me part."

"This is ridiculous!" Coyote cried. "I——"

"Wait!" Snake put in hopefully. "Let me settle the

quarrel. Now you roll the rock away. I'll take Mouse in
my coils just the way we were when Coyote came up.
We'll be then in a position to decide if——"

"Thank you," said Mouse. "It isn't necessary to trouble everyone again. Señor Coyote, we are even."

[CAMBODIA]

The Seed
of Happiness

Now it happened one day that a priest of Buddha was walking along the Mekong River deep in thoughts. Suddenly a woman came rushing out to meet him.

"Oh, Holy One," she cried. "No one in all the world has such troubles as I. Please help me. I have the most terrible troubles."

"Oh?" said the priest. "Now tell me true, woman. Are your troubles really terrible?"

"No, master," said the woman with a groan. "I only used the word terrible because there is no word in all the world strong enough to tell you how bad my troubles really are."

"It is indeed terrible when one's troubles are worse than terrible," the old man said, shaking his shaven head. "Suppose you tell me about them."

"Well, I was washing my clothes in the river when they caught on a floating branch and were lost. Then I was cooking supper and the rice pot turned over. My husband was angry at having no supper and beat me with a stick. I had a pet cat and he up and died yesterday. I had a pretty ring and I lost it. Oh, and there are so many other things I cannot remember them all, but I know I have more troubles than anybody."

"Yes," said the old priest, "I can see where someone like yourself might well consider these very terrible troubles indeed."

"Then please tell me how to stop having such terrible troubles," she said.

"When I was a boy in a village not far from here, I heard an old man once say that there is a sure way to make one's trouble go away," the old man said slowly. "I never tried it myself and I can only tell you what I heard."

"Oh, do tell me," she cried. "I will do anything to make myself rid of such terrible troubles as I have."

"This then is what I was told," the old priest said. "Go into the village and search until you find a house where those who live there have never had any troubles. Ask them for a single mustard seed. Take this seed to your own house and burn it. As the smoke of the mustard seed rises in the air, it will carry away all your troubles."

"Oh, and is that true?"

"I have heard it said," he replied.

"Then I will find me a mustard seed this very day!" she cried. "If what you have said is true, I will fill your bowl with rice every day as long as you live!"

"I will be sufficiently paid if you regain your happiness and lose your terrible troubles," he said.

Overjoyed, the woman rushed off to search for the house-with-no-troubles to get her precious mustard seed. The old priest went on his way.

The next day he happened to come by the same river path. He saw the woman carrying water from the stream. She was making an awful noise. At first he thought she was crying, but as he came closer he decided that she was singing. It was just that her voice was so bad her singing sounded awful.

"Well, good woman," the old priest said kindly, "I see that you are happy today. That must mean that you discovered a house-with-no-troubles and got your mustard seed."

"No, Holy One," she replied. "I went to every house in the village. In each one I found that the people inside had twice as many troubles as I had. I would not have believed it possible."

"Surely, you found one house without trouble for I heard you happily singing."

"No, it was just that I heard so many tales of woe that I was singing because I was happy that my troubles were no worse than they were."

"I am very happy to hear that," the old priest said. "You are now both a happier and a wiser woman."

[SPAIN]

A Salty Tale

Now it happened in Andalucia in Sunny Spain a long time ago that the Grand Duke Carlos had a servant named Juan who was as full of tricks as a bean pot is full of *frijoles*.

This sly youth was beaten at least ten times a day, but the whippings never cured him of playing tricks on everyone and everything.

Everyone said that someday the Grand Duke would become so angry with Juan that he would probably chop off the young man's head with one swish of his sword. And as it happened, the Duke was thinking of something almost as bad as that to cure Juan's trickery when the trickster pulled his strangest prank.

And did you know, that trick first made Duke Carlos so angry he almost exploded, then it made him astonished, and finally it made him so pleased that he gave Trickster Juan a bag of gold. He also ordered that from that day hence Juan could play as many tricks as he wished without punishment.

This is the way it happened:

The Grand Duke had no children of his own and took to live with him as his own the daughter of each of his three brothers. Sad to relate, two of the girls were very selfish, but the third was both generous and hard working.

Now it happened one afternoon when Juan was busy sweeping the garden walks that he heard Duke Carlos say to his three girls:

"I have a beautiful necklace of diamonds and rubies and pearls which belonged to your lovely aunt. It is the most beautiful necklace in the world and once long ago belonged to a queen. I have long wanted to give the necklace to you, but, alas, it is only one and you are three. Finally, I have decided to give it to the one who shows me that she loves me most. Now I want each of you to tell me how much you love your uncle so I can decide which one of you should have the jewels."

Rosita, who was lazy and selfish and spent all her time walking in the garden making flower garlands for her hair, said:

"Oh, my dear uncle! My love for you is as sweet as

the nectar of every flower in the world drained into one cup!"

This pleased Don Carlos. He then asked Carmen, the second girl, how much she loved him.

"My love for you, dearest uncle, is as sweet as all the honey in the world today, yesterday, and tomorrow!"

Carmen was also lazy and selfish. She loved nothing except eating. Don Carlos did not know this and was pleased by what she said. He then turned to the third girl, Manuela, and asked her how much she loved him.

"Dear uncle," she said, "I love you like salt."

"Like *what?*" the Grand Duke cried, looking at her in surprise.

"Like salt, dear uncle," the girl replied.

"Like common, everyday *salt!*" Don Carlos said angrily. "Then you cannot think much of me. Now you young ladies run along while I think about your stories and decide which loves me best."

He paused and looked angrily at Manuela. "I think," he added, "that I will only have to decide between two stories."

"But, uncle—" Manuela began tearfully.

"Please," Don Carlos said coldly. "It is too late to change your story. Run along now. I wish to think."

So the three girls left. Rosita and Carmen were laughing, but poor Manuela was in tears. Her uncle had not understood what she meant and she had not been permitted to explain.

Juan felt very sorry for her. He came over where Manuela was sitting on a garden bench, crying.

"But why did you tell him your love was like salt?" he asked. "Why didn't you do like the others and try to find the sweetest thing in the world?"

"But I only told the truth," Manuela said through her tears. "I really do love my uncle. I have been working in the kitchen to learn to cook and the cook told me how very important salt is. Flowers are pretty, but we do not need them to live. Honey is sweet, but you can't salt food with sugar."

"Ah!" cried Juan. "I understand now. When your uncle is told this he will understand also."

"But he will not listen," Manuela said, brushing at her tears with a dainty hand. "He told me to go away when I tried to explain."

"Then what you need is a trick!" Juan cried. "And His Smartness Señor Juan-the-Trickster is just the one to think of a good one!"

"Oh please, Juan! Do not make my uncle more angry than he is!" Manuela cried.

"This will not make him angry. It will make him see how wise you are, Señorita Manuela. For the first time in his life, Juan-the-Trickster is going to do a nice trick. I think I am as surprised at this as your uncle, the Grand Duke, is going to be!"

So Juan ran to his friend, the castle cook, for help. The cook, a gaint fat man, shivered when Juan told him what he wanted.

"Oh, no!" the cook cried. "Don Carlos will beat both of us if you try such a trick on him."

"But it is the only way I can make him see that it is really sweet Manuela and not the other two selfish girls who loves him best."

"Yes," the cook said, "Manuela is worth more than the two of them, but, Juan, I am afraid of the duke's anger."

"Then after it is over I will tell Don Carlos that it was all my fault and I will ask that I be whipped for both of us."

"Well, if you promise to do that—yes, for Manuela, I will help you!"

And so when the family came in for dinner that evening, Juan-the-Trickster brought in the soup and set it before Don Carlos. The duke took one spoonful and sputtered:

"*What* in the world is *this?*"

"Soup, sir," Juan said.

"Soup? Well, it tastes like something someone just washed the dog in. What is wrong with it?"

"It is your favorite soup, sir," said Juan. "I just left the salt out of it."

"Why did you do anything that silly?" the duke asked.

"But, sir, I thought from the way you yelled at Señorita Manuela, who said she loved you like salt, that you
no longer had any use for it."

"Well—" said Don Carlos angrily. "Take this stuff
away and bring in the fish."

When Juan brought in the fish, the duke took one
bite and threw down his fork.

"No salt, Juan?"

"No salt, my lord," said the trickster.

"Well, bring me some salt. I cannot eat this mess
without it!"

"I'm sorry, Don Carlos, but I thought you disliked
salt and so I gave all in the castle to Señorita Manuela.
She has the bag up in her room where she is even now
weeping her pretty eyes out because she has offended
you whom she loves like salt."

"Well, go get it from her. I cannot eat without salt."

"Very well, my lord. I will tell her that now you
understand what she meant when she said she loved
you like salt. I will tell her that you know now she
meant that she was low and humble even as salt is, but
that her love is so great that just a pinch of it can turn
the tasteless into something delightful even as a pinch
of salt can turn this mess in your plate into a fine roast."

"Juan," Don Carlos said severely, "you have tricked
me again. Do you remember what I said I'd do to you
for the next trick you played on me?"

"You promised to beat me, my Lord."

"Well, I take back that promise and will order the treasurer to give you a bag of gold for you have shown me that I was wrong to doubt the love Manuela had for me. You have taught me a lesson."

"And I, too, have learned a splendid lesson," Juan said, thinking happily of the bag of gold. "I learned that it is much better to play tricks that help someone instead of tricks that only make me laugh."

"Go," Don Carlos said. "You have my permission to play as many tricks of that kind as you wish."

Reynard and the Fisherman's Dream

Now it was late in the evening of a summer day when Monsieur Reynard-the-Fox decided he would have fish for his supper.

So he trotted down to the little stream which flows into the Seine not far from Paris. It was filled with fat fish. The fox could see them leaping from the water to catch the bug which skimmed low over the waves.

But it is not to be supposed that this famous French trickster bothered to cast out a line. Actually working for his food was unthinkable to this sly animal. He lived by his tricks and his wit.

So he paid no attention to the fish in the stream, but trotted along the bank until he saw a fisherman putting away his pole and line. A string of nice fat fish was hanging on the tree limb beside him.

"There," said the tricky fox, "is my supper."

He watched the fisherman put the string of fish in the back of his two-wheel cart and climb upon the seat.

"Get up," he said to the pony hitched to the cart. "We must get home before the moon rises."

Reynard watched the cart until it pulled into the deep-rutted road, the wheels squeaking and groaning as the pony pulled it over the rough way.

Then the fox ran down along the river bank until he was some way ahead of the fisherman's cart. Then he crept out into the road. He stretched out, opened his mouth, and turned his feet up to the sky.

Shortly he heard the creaking and groaning of the cart's wheels in the rough ruts. Then the noise stopped.

Reynard heard the fisherman say angrily, "Why have you stopped, little pony?"

He slapped the reins, but the pony refused to budge. The fisherman decided that something was barring the way, but it was hard for him to see in the gathering gloom. He got down off the seat and walked around in front of the pony.

It was then that he saw Monsieur Reynard stretched out on the road.

"Hoorah!" he said gleefully. "That tricky fox is dead at last. Now he can no longer steal my chickens."

He picked up the sly fox and brushed his hand over the thick red fur.

"Why, this is the most beautiful fur I have ever seen," he said. "I am sure that I can sell it for a large sum of money. This is wonderful luck!"

He threw the fox into the back of the cart beside the fish. Then he climbed onto the seat and started home again.

"Oh," he said happily, "I shall sell the fox's fur and with the money I'll buy a cow. Then the cow will have a calf and I will double my money. Then I'll sell them and buy a horse with the money. When the horse has a colt, I'll sell them and use the money to buy a new house!"

In the back Reynard was busily eating a fish. He nodded his head as he listened to the happy fisherman. "Yes," he said, "I guess he could do that."

He licked his chops and took another fish while the fisherman went on, "And I'll take boarders in my new house and make enough money to open a store!"

Reynard gulped down another fish and reached for still another. "Sure enough," he said, "the fisherman can do just as he says."

"And I am sure so many people will buy in my store that I will soon be rich. And when I am rich I will buy a beautiful castle to live in. I will have a hundred servants. I will no longer have to eat fish I catch and vegetables I grow. I will dine on banquets such as are set only on the tables of kings!"

Reynard had just finished the last fish. He licked his chops and stood up. He lightly tapped the fisherman on the shoulder. The surprised man turned his head.

Reynard said, "Since I am the cause of all your good fortune I think it only friendly that you invite me to come and eat at your banquet table!"

"Why—why——!" the fisherman cried. "You are supposed to be dead!"

"You may think so, but I don't!" said the fox with a laugh. He jumped down and started to run for the forest.

"Stop!" cried the fisherman. "Your fur belongs to me. Without it to sell I will lose everything!"

Reynard laughed and kept on running.

"You rascal!" cried the fisherman. "You are robbing me of my castle and my boxes of gold! You are the biggest thief in all the land! No one ever stole so much before!"

"Fine!" Reynard shouted back over his shoulder as he kept running. "Whatever I am, I like to be the best that is!"

The Weaver's Worry

Now there was once in Karachi a weaver who made cloth as soft as feathers, as warm as sheep's fleece, and which shimmered like gold.

The first time he made this wondrous cloth the weaver, Devadatta, sold it for one hundred pieces of gold. But that night his new wealth was stolen.

"Such is life," he said sadly, and went to his loom to make more cloth.

This piece was as wonderful as the first. He sold it for the same sum as the first. But that night the gold was stolen again.

The same thing happened again and again. Suddenly from a very ordinary weaver, Devadatta had become the greatest of them all. His wondrous cloth brought enough gold to buy him a castle if he could have kept it. But somehow, no matter how well he tried to hide the gold, it was always stolen. He only managed to keep enough to buy a few crusts of bread to keep from starving and to get new yarn for his loom.

When his gold vanished for the fifth time, the poor man decided that something was wrong. No thief, regardless of his cleverness, could have found the sly places where Devadatta had hidden his gold. He feared that somehow he had offended one or another of the many gods of his people. This god, he was sure, must be helping the thieves to find his hidden treasure.

As he was thinking over the problem, the chief of the Rajah's police sent for him.

"Our great master—On whom be Peace!—is very angry," the policeman said severely to the unhappy weaver.

"But, mighty one, what have I done?" Devadatta asked.

"You are the cause of Karachi having more thieves than any other spot in the kingdom," replied the policeman. "A man who is blamed for a single theft is sentenced to have his hands cut off. I don't know how we can find a suitable punishment for a man like you who is responsible for ten thousand thefts in a single week!"

"Ten thousand? *Me?* But, O mighty warrior of the Commander of the Faithful, I have never stolen anything in my life! Surely some enemy of mine has been telling terrible lies!"

"I did not say you had stolen anything!" the policeman cried. "Stop trying to confuse what is already confusing enough. I said you were responsible for so much property being stolen in Karachi. That is the same as stealing even if it should not be stealing itself."

"But, my lord, how could a poor weaver like me be in league with thieves. I assure your most gracious highness that if such were so, I'd be dressed in silk instead of rags and I'd be fat as the Rajah himself instead of half starved!" Devadatta protested.

"I did not say you were in league or helping the thieves plan their crimes," the policeman said testily. "What has happened is that the way you let your gold be stolen so easily has attracted the attention of every thief in the world! They are all headed for Karachi since they heard about you!"

"But is that my fault?" the poor weaver cried.

"Is it mine? Or the Rajah's? Whose else could it be but yours? These thieves come here and your gold is already stolen so they steal from the rest of us. Of course, it is your fault!"

And so the poor weaver was dragged off to the Rajah to stand trial for ten thousand acts of thievery.

Here Devadatta pleaded that all this was not his fault. Somehow he had offended some god or another. The Rajah looked at him closely.

"Somehow, I think I have seen you before," he said.

"O Pearl of Perfect Wisdom," the weaver said, "once I was your servant here in the palace, but you dismissed me because of the tricks I played on everyone."

"Ah, I remember now," the Rajah said. "You were much fatter in those days."

"Lord, I had more to eat then than now," the weaver said sadly.

"Sad to relate," the ruler replied, "but the Brahmins tell me that you are a victim of fate. It seems that you did a service for the god Krishna and a disservice for the god Bramah at the same time.

"Now in gratitude the one god gave to you the power to make the most wondrous cloth in the world so you would be paid like a king in gold. The other god, angry at your disservice, decreed that you could not keep the gold. He could not stop you from getting gold since that was the gift of Krishna, but he could stop you from keeping it. This is what all the trouble is about."

"Then, O Master of Perfection, all this is not my fault," the weaver said happily.

"Perhaps not, but I asked the old priests how long this mess will go on. They told me it would last as long as you lived. It seems to me that the thing to do is to see that you do not live any longer than *right now!*"

"O Merciful Lord! My life is worthless to you, but to me it is something precious. Now that I know what the trouble is let me try to find a way to stop all this. I was known as quite a trickster in my young days. Perhaps I can find a way."

"I do not think so," the Rajah said. "One god has decreed that you shall make much gold. Another has decreed that you shall not keep it. Even if they are sorry for what they have decreed, still they cannot change it for what is said is said and therefore must be. It is the same with the words of a ruler. I said you must die. Even if I regret my words, I cannot recall them now."

"Oh woe is me!" the poor weaver cried. "Will not anyone help me?"

"No one," said the Rajah.

"Then I must help myself," Devadatta replied.

"Do not think you can get out of this with some simple trick."

"Lord, I do not know what I am going to do, but I am going to do something. I do not have a pretty head, but I love what I have and wish it to stay on my shoulders."

"You can keep it if you prove wiser than both the gods and me," the Rajah said. "We have all spoken."

"But you passed the sentence of death on me only because you thought I would make more gold for more thieves to come and steal. If I do not do this anymore, then you do not need such a sentence of death."

"That is true. If you stop weaving, then I will not

have to carry out my sentence. But Krishna decreed that you will weave."

"Then I will weave as the one god decrees. I will lose the money as the other demands. I will confound the thieves as you insist. I will do exactly as all three of you wish."

"But it is impossible to do all three of these things," the Rajah said. "Impossible."

"If you will just let me try!"

"Very well, you may try, but if you are robbed one more time, your head will pay for it."

He wanted to stop weaving, but he could not for Krishna had decreed that he would turn out the world's most wondrous cloth. So he worked at the loom, skillfully threading fine lines of gold through the delicate colors of his fabric until the whole cloth shimmered like something alive.

As he neared the end, Devadatta was so frightened that he trembled all day and night. But even so he could not stop. Each day rich merchants came to see if he was finished and to offer heavy bags of gold for the living cloth. At the same time, the frightened weaver could see thieves lurking in the dark shadows ready to steal the gold from him.

He trembled some more. He knew what he had to do to save himself, but he was not sure that he could be swift enough to make the trick work.

Finally he could delay no longer. The cloth was finished. A buyer came and for two hours the two argued and bargained over a price.

"Why do you argue over a few copper coins extra?" the merchant cried. "As soon as you get the price, the gold will be stolen and you will die anyway! Come, give me a good bargain. It will not hurt you."

"A bargain is a bargain," Devadatta replied. "I must get the best price possible."

What he was really doing was delaying until the cool of the evening when many beggars came out on the streets. At the same time the shadows teemed with thieves hungry for his gold. He saw them but did not call the Rajah's police. It would have been useless. Suddenly, as a small beggar boy was passing by, Devadatta cried, "Sold!"

He threw the cloth in the surprised merchant's arms and grabbed the bag of gold. It was done so swiftly that all the thieves were taken by surprise also.

Devadatta rushed into the street and thrust the gold into the beggar boy's hands.

"A present!" he cried. "I pray you will remember me and give me a crust of bread and a skein of yarn in return!"

The boy shouted with joy and fled into the crowd ahead of the outraged thieves.

So it was that the weaver got the gold as one god decreed, lost it as another ordered, but still satisfied the Rajah by foiling the thieves.

And thus it happened every time thereafter. Suddenly the poor of Karachi started getting rich for each day Devadatta wove a new piece of cloth. And each day he gave it away to the poor. And these happy newly-rich brought him his bread and wine and yarn with which to weave more cloth.

This went on for years. Gradually the poor got rich, but the thieves starved. Devadatta could not keep his gold from being stolen for he was cursed by the angry god. The others could better protect their property and the thieves soon left for better pickings elsewhere.

So everyone in Karachi was happy. Even the weaver, for his continued gifts of gold made him a thousand friends, and he who has so many friends is wealthy even if his gold bag be empty of all but air.

The Stone Stew

It was eventide and the night was not far away. So the tramp whose name was Jack hurried to make the town of Banbury Cross, which is on the road to Londontown, before the darkness came.

As he approached the first house to beg for his supper, a voice called to him, "Ho, Jack, my old friend of the road!"

Jack turned and saw another tramp sitting under a tree with his little bundle of clothing beside him.

"Ho, Tom!" said Jack, "Come be about it, my friend. Let us find our supper at yonder house. I am so hungry I could even eat me, tough as I am!"

" 'Tis no good ye'll be doing in this stingy town,

Jack," Tom said sadly. "Every house I asked and I told many sad tales to account for my misfortune in this weary world. Not one heart did I touch. And yonder house which beckons you was the worst of them all. An old grandmother lives there alone. She has the temper of a dragon, the voice of a lion, and the strength of an elephant. She used them all on me, pounding my sore back with a broom until I fled from her yard."

"It sounds, my friend, as if this old granny does not like tramps."

"So it happens to be," Tom said. "And I hope you will recall the favor in later days that I have done you now. I have saved you the heavy blows of the old dragon's broom."

"Hmmm," Jack said. "Now you know, Tom, that a tramp is a tramp. He lives by begging his food. If he cannot beg, he starves."

"You tell me little that is new," his friend replied. "I know a tramp starves if he cannot beg his food for I am starving right now. I also know that I have company for you will starve with me."

"Poo! Not I," said Jack, "for I am the Prince of Tramps and a most sly fellow with a bag of tricks for every occasion—including old dragons who look like grandmothers! Now you watch and learn from a master. I will gather a supper for each of us and I will do it from that woman as payment for the broom beating she gave you, my friend."

"Jack, I agree that you are a very sly fellow, but no one is tricky enough to get a single crumb from that stingy old woman."

"As I say," retorted Jack, "stay hidden, but listen carefully and learn from a master!"

He went on jauntily down the road until he came to the house. The old woman was hoeing in her garden. Jack stopped and bowed to her. She looked up angrily from her work.

"You are a tramp!" she said, glaring at him.

"A Knight of the Road, madam," he said pleasantly. "And I was wondering if——"

"Not one bite, you no-good beggar! Just you wait until I get my broom. I'll have you on your way!" she cried.

"Please, madame!" Jack said. "Food is the last thing I need. What I wanted was that small white stone which you just turned up with your hoe. I am sure it is of no value to you since I noted you throwing out into the road all the rocks you turned up."

"Why do you want it?" she asked suspiciously.

Tom hesitated as if reluctant to give away a great secret. Finally he said, "I see you are a very smart woman so there is no use trying to fool you."

"You are absolutely correct, my man! Don't try to fool *me!*"

"Oh, I would never think of it!" Jack said quickly. "You are too wise for that. So I will tell you the truth.

That stone is just like the ones my mother used to use in making her famous stone stew. I wanted it to make one of my own. They are absolutely delicious!"

"What is a stone stew? I never heard of it."

"It is just about the most delicious stew in the world," Jack said. "And its recipe is a cherished secret in my family. So since the stone is of no value to you, will you please give it to me."

"I certainly will not! I will use it for my own stone stew!"

"Oh? Then you know the secret, too?" Jack asked.

"No," she admitted.

"I have had my supper so I am not hungry," Jack said slyly. "Otherwise I would stop and show you the secret of the stone stew since you remind me of my grandmother, dear old lady that she is."

"Perhaps you could tell me," the old woman suggested.

"No, the secret is in the way the stone is used in the stew," Jack replied. "I would have to show you. It is a wonderful secret. I recall that after my mother learned it, everyone said she was the best cook in the township. I'm sure everyone here would say the same of you if you knew the secret."

"I always wanted to be the best cook in town," the old woman said wistfully. "Everyone thinks my sister is now and how she lords it over me. I get angry every time I think of it."

(*116*)

"Then I will help you," Jack said quickly. "I notice you have a pot of beef meat cooking on the stove. Now you take this stew stone and wash it very clean and put it in the pot with the meat so the stone flavor can mix well with the juices."

"Yes, yes!" the old woman said eagerly. "Now what do I do?"

"Now put in one of the fine tomatoes growing in your garden. Then add a potato. Do you have an onion and a carrot?"

"This sounds just like a regular stew to me," the old woman said.

"Ah, but the secret flavor comes from using the stew stone," Jack said. "Now just a pinch of salt, if you please."

He stirred the bubbling pot and dipped out a spoonful to sip.

"The secret of good cooking," he told the old woman, "is to taste the dish as it cooks so you will know how it is coming on."

Well, the stone stew seemed to be coming on very well for Jack kept tasting and tasting and tasting until he had tasted up half the pot.

"Let me taste it," the old woman said.

"Oh, it isn't quite done yet," Jack said hastily.

But before he could stop her she grabbed a spoon and took a bite of the stew.

"I can't taste any difference between your stone stew

and my regular stew," she said suspiciously, as she reached for her broom.

"One must get used to the difference in taste," Jack said quickly. "Let me show you."

He stepped to the window and called to Tom. When the other tramp came running, Jack said, "Now, sir, I take it that you are a lover of stone stew. So sit down here and taste this fine dish and tell me what you think of it."

He placed a brimming bowl in front of his friend. Tom started to eat greedily for he was half starved.

"See!" Jack cried. "Why I happen to know that this fine fellow wasn't the least bit hungry, but look how he devours this delicious stew! That is proof that the flavor is superb! Madam, with this stew stone you will be known as the greatest cook in Banbury Cross!"

"Well, he does look as if he is enjoying it greatly," she said.

"I see, sir," Jack said to Tom, "that you have emptied your bowl. Come let us be off and not keep this fine woman from her meal."

He bowed low as if she were a queen, and skipped out the door with Tom right behind him.

"What a fine fellow!" the old lady said. "Now I will have a bowl of my new stone stew myself."

But when she went to the pot there was nothing left in it but the smooth stew stone. The two tramps had eaten every bite of the rest!

[EGYPT]

The Greedy Friend

It happened, O *effendi*, that once there were two friends and they came down to the wondrous city of Cairo to make their fortunes.

Both men worked very hard, but money did not come easy to them. So it was that seven years passed before either man had anything like wealth.

At the end of the seven years the two men still worked together. Their friendship, however, had long since cooled. Banta, an honest man, had seen enough to convince himself that his former friend, Anpu, was a rascal. The man was greedy, miserly, and when he could do so without danger, a thief.

So it was that when Banta received word that his

father was ill in Memphis, the honest man made plans to go home for a visit. There were no banks in those days. Men going on journeys usually left their money with friends or with moneylenders whom they trusted. As it happened, Banta trusted no moneylender and he trusted his so-called friend, Anpu, even less.

He did not dare risk taking with him any more gold than just enough for the journey. There were bandit bands along the route.

Finally he decided to hide the money in the ground. He and Anpu still shared the mud hut by the Nile River where they had lived since coming to Cairo. So while Anpu was asleep that night Banta carefully dug a hole in the floor in the spot where his sleeping quilt was usually stretched.

He dug very quietly with many anxious glances across at his untrustworthy friend. Anpu did not open his eyes, but kept snoring loudly. Sure that no one had seen him bury the money in the hole, Banta carefully replaced the dirt and spread his quilt back over the spot. He then went to sleep himself.

The next morning he informed Anpu that he was going to Memphis.

"At first," he said, "I intended to leave my little bag of gold with you since you are my friend. Then I decided to take it with me since I may need to pay for my father's doctor."

"I think you are doing a very wise thing," Anpu said.

Banta did not see the sly way his false friend darted a look with his eyes at the spot where the tiny wealth of seven year's work was buried. Anpu had not been asleep at all when Banta buried his money.

Banta was gone for thirty days. When he returned he rushed straight for the house to see if his money was still safe. Anpu, he learned, had gone down the river for two days to trade for papyrus reeds. He hastily dug to the bottom of the hole.

His money was gone.

Roaring with rage, he rushed off through the market-place to the *cadi*, who is the wise judge who hears complaints of the wronged.

"O Most Honorable Cadi," Banta cried. "My false friend, Anpu, dug up the four gold pieces I hid in the mud floor of our house while I dutifully visited my sick father in Memphis. May Your Honor—On Whom Be Peace!—cause the rascal to be dragged to the city square and have his hands chopped off as is fitting and proper for a wicked thief!"

"Oh?" said the cadi, who was very famous for the oddity of his judgments. "And why do you accuse your friend, Anpu? Did a witness see him steal your gold?"

"No, Illustrious One," said Banta. "But he was sleeping in the room when I buried the money. He pretended to be asleep, but he was spying on me!"

"If you knew he was spying on you, why did you leave the money in the hole for him to take?" the great judge asked.

"But I did not know then that he was only pretending to sleep," Banta said. "I did not know that until I came back and found my money gone."

"Oh?" said the cadi as he thoughtfully stroked his long gray beard. "What street did you walk when you came back to the city from Memphis?" he asked.

"I walked along the street of the Camel Drovers, *effendi*."

"There was a bold robbery about that time in this street. Could it be that you are that thief?"

Banta's face turned pale. "O Heavens! My Lord! I know nothing of any robbery."

"But you were in the street when this robbery happened," the cadi said severely.

"But that does not make me a thief," Banta said, his knees shaking.

"No," said the cadi, "and neither does it make Anpu a thief because he was in the room where your gold was stolen. Before I can chop off his hands, as is fitting and proper to punish a thief, you must bring me more proof than you have."

Tears came to Banta's eyes. He realized what had happened. Somehow Anpu had bribed the judge. Seven years of hard work were lost. Worse, there was a good chance if he continued to complain that the judge would have Banta thrown in jail. His head dropped. His shoulders sagged. He spread his hands helplessly and turned to go.

The cadi let him get almost to the door. Then he said, "Come back here."

There was a note in his voice that made Banta tremble even more. He was sorry now that he had ever complained about his lost gold.

The cadi looked at him most severely and then said, "I can read minds. Did you know that, Banta?"

The frightened man shook his head. The cadi said, "And I will tell you what is in your mind right now: You think that Anpu gave me a gold piece to refuse to listen to your complaint when you found your money gone. Is that not true?"

"L-l-lord, I-I——" Banta was too frightened now to speak. He could see the cadi having him shut up in prison for life to keep the world from knowing that he had taken gold from Anpu to decide the case for him.

"Well, if that is what you think," the cadi said with a chuckle of amusement, "you would be *right!* He came to me right after he stole your gold and offered me one gold piece as my share. In return I must refuse to listen to your complaint. I took the gold and I refused to listen. You can see that I made a bargain with Anpu and I kept that bargain."

Poor Banta now knew that he would surely die. Having confessed that he took a bribe, the cadi could not permit him to live and tell others of the crime. He groaned in his misery.

The curious cadi smiled at Banta's misery.

"You may wonder why I took Anpu's gold and why I tell you about it," the odd judge said, chuckling happily in his deep beard. "I tell you for several reasons.

"One, I think our punishment of cutting off a man's hands is too severe even for a faithless friend and thief like Anpu.

"Second, I know an old woman who is starving and needs help.

"Third, I am very proud of my honesty and the fairness of my judgments.

"Fourth, I think you have been wronged when you lost your gold.

"These then are the reasons I took the gold piece Anpu offered me and promised not to sentence him to the chopping block for his crime. Do you not think I acted wisely?"

Banta was frightened, but he was also angry. He knew he must die anyway, so what he said now could not hurt him.

"No!" he cried. "How can you call it acting wisely when you rob me and let a thief escape punishment?"

"I didn't say he would escape punishment," the cadi replied and chuckled again. "I just said I promised he would escape the traditional punishment of a thief.

"Now you have doubted my wisdom. That itself is a crime and I must sentence you. You are to stand here beside me when Anpu comes back to find out what happened when you complained. Then when he stands outside the door listening to us, you will act as if you did not yet know that your gold is gone.

"You will tell me that you returned from Memphis with two more pieces of gold which were left to you when your father died. You will say so Anpu can hear that you intend to return to your home here in Cairo tonight, and bury these two new coins with the four you placed there before. You will then wait here for a half hour. After that go home and dig open the hole where you hid the money before.

"If I am not badly mistaken, you will find that your four coins have returned."

Banta did as the cadi ordered. Sometime after that he came rushing back to the court.

"O Great Cadi!" he cried. "You were right. My money returned!"

"Of course," the cadi said, smiling. "I knew that when Anpu heard that you intended to place more gold in the hole, he would return your money. You see, he is a very greedy man. He knew if you found the hole empty you would not put more money into it. He thought by returning the four gold pieces, you would put the other two in and he could come back and get all six.

"Now since he already had given me one gold piece, he had to take one of his own to make up the four.

"So you got your money back. I got one gold piece

which I shall give to the old woman I mentioned who needs money to keep from starving. And Anpu loses one gold coin.

"Since you lost nothing, Anpu cannot be a thief and I cannot order his hands cut off. He tried to be a thief and for this he paid with his lost gold coin.

"So it is that you won for you have your money back. The old woman wins for she now has money to buy food. And I win because I was honest and did for Anpu what I promised in return for his bribe: I saw that he was not punished for stealing. But at the same time I had him punished for trying to steal—which is something else.

"Now go your way and live in happiness for you are protected by the wisest judge in the world—me, of course."

[JAPAN]

The Way of the Master

Once it happened that the ruler of Japan called his most trusted servant, Okubo Hikozaemon, to come to the palace.

"Okubo," he said, "a disturbing report has come to me from a little village back in the mountains. I want you to do something about it."

"Lord, I will go up and chop the heads off a few of them and I promise you the rest will behave," the old warrior said.

"No, no!" the ruler said. "Had I wanted that I have a thousand warriors I could have sent and not have had to disturb your well-earned rest. I need a sly man for this job. It seems to me that an old trickster like you is just the man for the job."

"Lord," said old Okubo, "what is the job?"

"There is a village called Mimura set far back in the mountains. The roads are steep and rugged. It is very hard to get to this place. So it happens that the people of the village never travel anywhere. Neither does anyone go to visit them. The way is too hard."

"Yes, my Lord," Okubo said. "I know of the village of Mimura."

"Well," said the ruler, "I learned two years ago that the people of Mimura were very backward since they never visited or were visited by others. This saddened me for I wish all of my people to be well taught.

"So I sent out a teacher to instruct them in the changing ways of the world for they were a hundred years behind the times."

"Our master is very wise," Okubo said.

"I *thought* so myself," the ruler said peevishly. "But as it happened, I was not. I wanted to send a good teacher. So I recalled the one who instructed me in my lessons so many years ago. He is too old for such an arduous journey, of course. But he has a son and I thought he would have the wisdom of his father. I dispatched him to the village."

"He is not as learned?"

"He is more learned than his father. He knows more from books than his father, you and I, all put together.

Unfortunately, he is an educated idiot. All he knows is what his books say. If it isn't in a book, he does not believe it so. If it isn't written down, it is not right to him."

Okubo shook his head. "Such a man would be a poor teacher for a backward village," he said.

"That I know," the ruler said. "They will only change one wrong way of doing things for another. I wish them to learn many ways."

"Then why not replace the teacher with a wiser one who understands that there is more than what is written in books." Okubo asked.

"My regard for my old teaching master is so great that I can not cause him to lose face as he would if I had to recall his son," the ruler said. "So all you have to do is convince him that he should give up the teaching job. Then when he asks me to retire, I can get rid of him without offending his old father. It is very simple."

Okubo scratched his bald head. He had served the ruler and his father before him. Because he had been in the *Shogun's* service for so long, he was permitted to say things to the ruler that would have gotten the head of a lesser man chopped off.

"Lord," he said, "if I may be permitted to disagree, the job is not simple at all. Had it been you would not have sent for me. For sixty-five years—since I was twelve years old—I have served your House of Tokugawa. In that time I have done ten thousand jobs. Not one was simple. They were all something so distasteful or so difficult that no one else could or would do them. What is wrong with this one?"

The Shogun—for that was the ruler's title—smiled. "I have sent men to the village to hint to the young man that he should resign, but he is so filled with self-importance that he cannot take the hints. He is very proud of the fact that he is the model for the people of his village and that he has taught them to do just as he does."

"Oh? said old Okubo. "So they do *just* as he does?"

"So I am told," said the ruler.

"That should make my task simple after all," Okubo said with the hint of a smile. "I shall need a few items to assist me."

"Ask for what you will," the Shogun said.

"Then send with me a barrel of wine, two big baskets of potatoes, a *koku* of rice, six baskets of fruits and vegetables, two sacks of sugar, and sufficient money to buy a hundred fish at the local market."

"This is ridiculous!" the Shogun snapped. "I am willing to provide you food for the journey, but this is enough for a banquet!"

"That is just what I intend to have," said the old man. "A banquet which I hope will teach our 'do-like-me' friend a good lesson in manners!"

So it was that Okubo Hikozaemon went up in the mountains with a train of porters carrying provisions for a great banquet. When he arrived at the village he immediately sent for the teacher who was named Tadasuke.

"Tadasuke," he said, "I understand that you have brought these villagers out of their backwards ways."

"I have labored mightily, Honorable Okubo," the young man said. "Many times I have been sorely tried, but at last I have everyone behaving properly."

"Which, I understand," Okubo said slyly, "is just as you behave."

"I have tried to be a model to my people," the young teacher replied.

"And they do just exactly as you do?" the old man asked.

"Simply because I have made myself a model for them."

"Well!" Okubo said. "I have never before seen a model people. I shall give a banquet for all of them. Have them at the inn where I am staying at twilight time tonight. Be sure that they behave properly since I am giving this banquet in the name of the Shogun himself. It will be an offense to the ruler in Yedo if they do not conduct themselves well."

"Oh, there will be no trouble," the young man replied. "After all these people are only country bumpkins and are not intelligent like us folk from the city. So, I have carefully instructed them to always watch me when they go to public functions and do *exactly* as I do."

"*Exactly?*" Okubo said, looking pleased.

"*Exactly!*" the teacher said, his face showing his pride in his wise methods of teaching the countrymen.

"Then things should go at the party exactly as I had hoped," Okubo said slyly. "Oh, *exactly!*"

And so it happened that all the men of the village came to the banquet given by Okubo Hikozaemon in the name of the great Shogun who ruled Japan for the Emperor in Kyoto.

Okubo sat on a raised platform at the end of the room. Cushions had been placed on the floor for the guests to sit in front of little low tables upon which the dishes for the banquet were already in place.

The guests came in and knelt in their places. They all turned to watch their teacher. He bowed very low to Okubo and said, "We are honored and grateful that your excellency has——"

He stopped in surprise as all the others bowed and started to parrot his words: "We are honored and grateful that your excellency has——"

The young teacher's face turned red. He had told them to do exactly as he did, but he had meant his table manners. He didn't expect them to parrot every word he said.

"We are honored and grateful," he began again. And

at the same time he made a little waving motion of his hand to try and let them know that they were not supposed to repeat his words.

His face turned even redder when he saw every villager in the room made the same motion as they repeated his words.

On his dais Okubo Hikozaemon had difficulty keeping from bursting out in laughter. He managed it though and stared solemnly at the flustered teacher.

He said, "Let us give thanks to the Emperor and the Shogun in whose names we dine here tonight."

He raised his O-hashi—chopsticks—as a signal for them to begin to eat. The poor embarrassed teacher darted his eyes around to see how his students were behaving. In his nervous anxiety he did not watch his own food. The rice ball in its brown soy sauce which he was raising to his mouth missed his lips and bumped against his nose!

He knew before it happened what his students would do. He groaned in horror as each one touched his nose with the sauce covered rice ball, and then groaned exactly as he had.

This was too much. He staggered to his feet, his face crimson with embarrassment, and bowed clumsily to Okubo.

"I am so sorry, Okubo-san," he said shakily. "But I-I-I am v-very sick. If you will excuse me!"

He rushed out of the house. Behind him the villagers

looked sadly at the food they would miss and said, "I am so sorry, Okubo-san. But I-I-I am v-very sick. If you will excuse me!"

They rushed out of the house the same way their teacher had done. As they left Okubo heard one say, "I always thought one got something to *eat* at banquets."

The old warrior laughed for a while and then had his servants divide up the food and carry it to the houses of the villagers. Then he went to see the crestfallen teacher. He found the young man in tears and packing to leave.

"Where are you going?" Okubo asked kindly.

"Away," the young man said bitterly. "Ten thousand miles away, and I will never try to be a teacher again."

"I think that would be a mistake," Okubo said. "You have the learning to make a very fine teacher. Don't let the little trick I arranged for you change your life's work. I only wanted to prove to you that it is a dangerous thing to insist on everyone doing exactly as you do. Your job is to teach them what is right and let them do it their own way—for there are many ways of doing things. I think now that you know this, you can start over and be a fine teacher, indeed."

The young man did and became a very fine teacher, indeed.

The Onion and the Rose

Now in the days long ago when good King Chung Jong ruled Korea there was a very wise, but somewhat tricky judge named Im Bang who held court in Suwon city.

Now it happened that Im Bang had been away from Suwon for several weeks on a mission for the king. When he returned the first villager who came to see him wept and cried that his daughter was going to be killed by the royal swordsman.

"You must be mistaken," Im Bang said kindly. "I know your daughter. Since she was a child I have never seen a better behaved little girl. I am sure she would do nothing to cause the king to have her killed."

"It is not my daughter," the old man said, weeping so

hard the judge could scarcely hear his words. "It is Wol Mai."

"You mean that rich old woman who causes us so much trouble?" Im Bang asked. "She is worse than a dragon. What has she done now?"

"For years this wicked creature has been cheating everyone," the old man said. "Each time she is caught she manages to put the blame on someone else. When she cheated on her taxes, she blamed her chief clerk and he was put to death in her place. When she was caught giving short measure in her store, she blamed a servant and he was whipped in her place. And so on and on many times others paid for her crimes and sins. Why, even as a child, the servant's children were punished when Wol Mai was naughty. Someone else has always taken the blame for her."

"I know," Im Bang said. "But she is so clever no one has been able to catch her until lately. I found proof and sent it to the king in Seoul. He has ordered her to be placed in prison for the rest of her life."

"Oh, but that is the trouble, Judge Im Bang," the old man said. "Lately our house has fallen on sad days. To keep from starving, we sent my daughter to work as a servant in Wol Mai's house. Yesterday the old dragon got word from a spy that the king had ordered her put in prison for the rest of her life. So she ordered my daughter to exchange garments with her and go in her place to prison. You know that women in prison wear heavy veils to hide their shame. So none would know of the exchange."

"Your daughter should have refused," the judge said.

"Wol Mai threatened to have me thrown in prison if my daughter did not take her place. She claimed she would tell the police I stole some gold from her. To save me, my daughter agreed to go to prison in Wol Mai's place."

"So?" Im Bang said. "What do you want me to do?"

"Please stop Wol Mai from forcing my daughter to exchange clothes with her."

"I cannot do that," Im Bang said thoughtfully. "Wol Mai has been blaming her servants for her crimes so long that it has become a custom in Suwon. You do not want me to change an old custom, do you?"

"But, honorable Im Bang!" the old man said. "I——"

"Let me hear no more! What is to be, will be. Go home and do not trouble me again."

Within an hour the whole town knew that Im Bang had refused to save the poor girl. Then those who had loved the old judge now hated him. They thought that he had taken Wol Mai's gold to save her from prison and sent the little maid in her place.

And so on the next day the young girl, wearing the rich robes of Wol Mai and with a heavy veil over her face, was led to the prison gate. With her came the old woman wearing the servant girl's clothing. She, too, wore a heavy veil.

Im Bang, as the judge, met them at the prison gate. "Are you Wol Mai?" he asked the little maid.

"Yes, she is," the old woman said quickly before the girl could speak.

"You have no family, Wol Mai," Im Bang said to the girl. "Who will look after your home and your fortune while you spend the rest of your life in prison?"

"I will do it for her," the old woman said eagerly.

"No," Im Bang said. "For fifty years Wol Mai has been blaming others for what she did and they have always taken her punishment for her. This has happened so long that it has become a custom. I will not change an old custom. Jailer, take this servant woman and put her in prison in Wol Mai's place!"

The prison guards grabbed Wol Mai who was in the servant's clothing.

"Wait!" the old woman cried. "I am really Wol Mai. She is the servant. Jail her!"

"Impossible," Im Bang said. "Servants do not wear such rich clothing."

He turned to the large crowd of people gathered around them.

"Have any of you good people ever seen a servant so richly dressed?"

"No! Oh, no, honorable Im Bang!" they cried, delighted at the way things were turning out.

"Neither have I," said the old judge. "Throw this servant in the darkest cell and never let her out."

And when they led her away and Im Bang could no longer hear the old dragon's shouts of rage, the judge turned to the little maid who wore the rich clothes of Wol Mai.

"And as for you, Wol Mai," he said, "I charge you to change your ways of the past. Go home and use your great wealth to help your fellow men and women of Suwon."

And as it happened, she did just that.

Author's Notes
on Story Sources

1. Sissa and the Troublesome Trifles

This is a story told to me in India by a shopkeeper who specialized in chess sets. There is quite a variety of stories about the origin of chess.

2. Ikkyu and the Merchant's Moneybags

A very free adaptation from a children's folk song about the famous thirteenth century Buddhist priest. In the original the climax depends upon a pun which cannot be translated and make sense. There are a great number of Japanese children's stories about Ikkyu, which teach Buddhist moral lessons by personifying Ikkyu as Good and the rich merchant as Evil. Because so many of them depend upon puns and other features which lose their humor in translation, Ikkyu is one of the few folk heroes of the world who has not found his way into English language folktale collections.

3. Agayk and the Strangest Spear
This is an Eskimo tale changed slightly to eliminate considerable bloodthirstiness.

4. Geordie and Ten-Shilling Jock
I have heard this tale attributed also to Robert Burns, the poet, who has become himself a folk hero in Scotland.

5. Hodja and the Jumbled Jobs
The Hodja is a favorite Near East hero. I chose this particular story—told to me originally by a Turkish soldier who served with the Turkish United Nations troops in Korea—because it was not included in either Kelsey's *Once the Hodja* or in Ramsay and McCullagh's *Tales From Turkey*, the two best-known sources of Hodja tales in English. There is a somewhat similar story in Japanese attributed to the historical-folk hero, Okubo Hikozaemon.

6. Tyl's Task
Tyl Eulenspiegel is one of the better-known folk heroes. This story follows the line of a couple of folklore motifs known worldwide and usually featuring local heroes.

7. The Just Judgment
Abu al Nawas is a staple Iranian folk hero. This particular tale is also known in other countries of the Far East, and especially resembles some of the tales told of Karakousch, the fantastic Egyptian judge.

8. Ooka and the Telltale Tale
This is taken from *Solomon in Kimono*, the author's book, published in Japan in 1956.

9. The Silly Slave
A story very freely adapted from Aesop's Fables.

10. Señor Coyote
A tale attributed in various countries to every folk hero from Solomon to Brer Rabbit.

11. The Seed of Happiness
Known throughout Indo-China, this is often attributed to Buddha himself.

12. A Salty Tale
I have heard versions of this story all over Europe. Shakespeare used a version in *King Lear*.

13. Reynard and the Fisherman's Dream
A well-known French tale.

14. The Weaver's Worry
A story taken from the author's "Destiny's Debt," published in *Stars and Stripes*.

15. The Stone Stew
A familiar folktale known in many countries.

16. The Greedy Friend
A similar tale is attributed to King Solomon, who advises that the money be reburied. This is also known as an Ooka story in Japan.

17. The Way of the Master
This is a popular Japanese folktale under its original title, "The Rolling Potatoes." Apparently Okubo Hikozaemon was a later addition to an older tale.

18. The Onion and the Rose
A Korean story of unknown origin. Im Bang was a famous writer of folktype tales about one or two hundred years ago.